ROTTERS

BRAVO COMPANY

CARL R. CART

SEVERED PRESS
HOBART TASMANIA

ROTTERS

Other Books By This Author:

MORE ZOMBIES THAN BULLETS

ROTTERS

ROTTERS: ALPHA CONTACT

DWARFS OF THE DEAD

DETOUR 366

ZOMBIEMEISTER 9

Acknowledgements

Rotters Bravo Company was only made possible by the generous help of my very good friends Captain David West Reynolds and Jack A. Bobo.

Captain Dave and I shared many hours discussing the fate of Bravo Company. Dave came up with the horrors of the Sample Tent.

Jack, or as I call him, Tony, is the first to read my rough drafts and provide me with critical analysis of my stories.

My works are always made better by the help of these two scoundrels.

Matt Bliss, who once again provided military intelligence.

I would like to thank Gary and the staff of Severed Press; this book and the series would not exist without them.

My friend Jamey Aebersold always helps me with formatting and proofreading.

Another close friend, Kelly Pitt, generously assists me with his printing expertise and first runs on rough drafts.

Finally, my thanks to my wife, Jennifer, who always reads my stories, and tries not to think too hard about the inner workings of my twisted mind.

For the sake of my readers who are not familiar with military ranks and language. A person in the military can be called by their rank alone (Sergeant, Major, etc.), or by their last name (considered disrespectful of senior NCOs and officers), or frequently by a nickname (often derogatory). Note also that even though Colonel Warren outranks Major Dorset, Dorset is technically the commanding officer of Bravo Company. Commanding officers are typically known as the CO. As the senior noncommissioned officer (NCO), Master Sergeant McAllister is in command of both platoons, under the authority of the company's officers. Senior NCOs are often more experienced than officers, and may be unofficially in command. Almost everyone in the military gets a nickname at some point.

This book is dedicated to every man and woman who ever found themselves in a trench or foxhole.

PROLOGUE

04:35 a.m. Zulu
Village of Mumban
Democratic Republic of Congo

Micca bolted upright in her narrow bed and looked around in terror. She wasn't sure what had awakened her until she heard the screams begin again. She leapt from the bed and pulled on her thin dress and old sneakers. Pausing only long enough to grab up her late father's burnoose, she bolted into the street and ran headlong for the forest.

She ran for her life through a bedlam of fire and massacre. The village was going up in flames all around her. The leaping conflagration threw long, grotesque shadows upon the thatch hut walls. The mud streets ran red with blood, and butchered, headless bodies lay in heaps in all directions. Smoke drifted on the breeze, carrying the smell of burning meat. The stuttering bark of an AK-47 sounded nearby. Micca flinched, and ran faster. She knew that sound all too well.

Terror almost overwhelmed her. She forced herself to stop as she reached the last hut at the edge of the village. A clearing fully one-hundred meters wide lay between her and the safety of the rain forest. Micca lay on her stomach and wiggled forward until she could cautiously peer around the hut's thatch wall. Her eyes widened with fear as she witnessed the horrors before her. She jammed her knuckles into her mouth to stop her sobs.

Rebel soldiers walked calmly around the perimeter of the burning village, guns in hand. Micca stifled a scream as two small children ran from the ruins. Three soldiers fired into their tiny bodies, mowing them down in a hail of bullets. One of the killers stalked forward, a machete in hand. He knelt down and brutally decapitated the murdered children. The monster calmly stood and carried their severed heads to the edge of the wood. He and another

1

soldier jammed the heads onto sharpened wooden poles, and set them upright into the ground next to the other grizzly, dripping trophies already there.

In growing horror, Micca realized there were dozens of them in a circle surrounding the burning village. The soldiers turned from their work, and as she watched, the small headless bodies were tossed back into the burning buildings. Tears blurred her vision.

The thatch pressed against her stomach suddenly grew painfully warm. Micca squirmed away from the wall as small tongues of flame burst through the thin wooden wall. Smoke stung her, and the heat began to become unbearable. She could barely breathe. Micca held on as long as she could; finally, the torment was too great.

She sprang to her feet and ran for the tree line; her long legs flashed in the firelight. From the corner of her eye, she registered the muzzle flash; then darkness reached out and took her.

CHAPTER 1

10:15 a.m.
Emergency Medical HQ
Village of Lat, the Congo

Colonel Ortega could feel his control of the situation slipping away, inch by inch. Everything that could go wrong had gone wrong; Murphy's Law was in full effect. Chaos lurked just below the thin layer of organization that the colonel was managing to maintain. Ortega ran his fingers through his thinning hair, and exhaled loudly. Files and reports covered every inch of his makeshift desk, and the uneaten remains of his last meal sat untouched on a plastic tray. He was running on cold coffee and sheer stubbornness.

Ortega had brought his small medical unit to this forsaken village three days ago with specific orders. It was his mission to stop a viral outbreak, an epidemic that had decimated the indigenous population, and quickly spread beyond the local government's ability to counter or control. The virus was unlike anything Col. Ortega had ever encountered. Every single member of the small village had contracted the disease, except for the handful that had fled into the surrounding forest. Roughly a hundred moaning victims of the virus were spread throughout the village's tiny clinic and the Army tents surrounding the HQ. None of Ortega's staff had become infected yet, but the colonel knew it was a grim possibility. They were losing a race against time.

Ortega was sure that the virus was being transmitted by fluidic contact, he hadn't ruled out aerosol transmission either. He and his staff wore protective gear at all times outside the clean command laboratory tent, and followed all standard decontamination protocols.

The virus was extremely fast acting and caused death through high fever and resultant brain damage. Although they had identified the virus, it had so far proved resistant to any counter measures. It seemed to be something entirely new. The colonel was at a loss. All of the modern equipment at his disposal, all of the protocols, all of his work... none of it seemed to matter. The virus was winning.

A makeshift morgue had been set up in the village's church. The priest was in no condition to complain; he had been one of the first casualties. The locals had been burning the dead before the unit's arrival. Ortega quickly put a stop to the practice, over the objections of the village elders. At first, he had needed some of the bodies for autopsies, now there were far too many to bury or burn. They were stacked like cord wood inside the small chapel. Hardened as he was to death, Ortega could barely manage to approach the morgue. The flies and the stench had become absolutely horrific. Africa was not a pretty place to die.

The colonel had just gone back to preparing a report when his second-in-command entered the lab. Ortega continued to type as Captain Forsythe approached his desk.

"Sorry to bother you, sir, but we have a serious problem," the captain reported.

Ortega looked up. The captain's face looked grim. His second wasn't given to exaggeration. "Another problem? What is it now?" he replied.

"You had better come see this for yourself," Forsythe said curtly.

"You can't just tell me?" Ortega asked.

"No, sir, you wouldn't believe me," the captain answered.

The officers suited up and left the laboratory tent. As they stepped outside, the heat hit Ortega like a physical blow, and he began to sweat immediately. The suit was stifling and constricting on a good day; the African heat made working in the protective suits almost unbearable.

Capt. Forsythe led Ortega through the deserted village to the chapel. They stopped before the front steps. The small church's foyer looked like a slaughterhouse floor. The front door hung askew by one twisted hinge, and blackened blood covered the wooden floorboards and the rough plank walls. Thousands of bloated black flies covered the church in a crawling, buzzing mass.

The colonel looked around in puzzlement.

"Where are the bodies?"

"We honestly don't know, sir," Forsythe replied.

"The villagers must have taken them out to burn them," Ortega suggested.

"I thought that at first too, sir, but there aren't any villagers left capable of that," the captain reported sadly.

"What?" the colonel queried.

"All of the villagers are sick or dead, sir; all of them," Forsythe answered.

"Why would outsiders come into the village to remove these bodies?" Ortega asked.

"They didn't," the captain offered. "Look at the footprints, sir."

Ortega walked slowly around the chapel's entry. All of the bloody footprints came out of the church; there were no prints going in. The colonel knelt down and scanned the muddy ground closely. All of the prints led outward, into the forest.

"There are no drag marks either, sir," Forsythe observed dryly.

"What are you suggesting?" Ortega asked.

"I don't know," the captain replied. "I just don't know."

CHAPTER 2

2:44 p.m. Zulu
Village of Umjebec
Ethiopia, Africa

"I fucking hate Africa and I hate Africans!" PFC Harde grumbled as he struggled to load another fifty-pound bag of rice onto the light cargo truck.

"That's okay," I laughed. "I'm pretty sure Africa hates you back."

"Fuck you, Parsons," Harde replied wearily.

"He doesn't mean anything personal by that, Gordo," I added in apology to our interpreter. Gordo was assigned to our squad; he was a college grad who could speak about a dozen of the local dialects. Technically, he was a civilian contractor assigned to our company. Ironically, his family had immigrated to the United States to get away from Africa, but once he opted to work for the Army, they sent him right back. He was sharp as hell, but he wasn't quite as crude as the rest of the grunts. Gordo was a good guy. He didn't just talk; he worked hard and pulled his weight.

"It's alright," Gordo grunted as he threw a bag into the truck. "Africa is not for white men," he laughed.

"Fuck in A' right," Harde agreed. "It's too damn hot all the damn time."

I had to agree with Harde, or as we called him, Hard-on, on that one. I was originally from Detroit, and hadn't stopped sweating since I had stepped off the plane. Our company had been deployed from Afghanistan to help with humanitarian aid and emergency food distribution after a bad drought in Africa. We had bounced from one Third World shit-hole to another one.

All we had done in Ethiopia was load fucking rice onto trucks by the motherfucking ton. Either that or stand guard and sweat while the other guys in the company loaded rice.

6

Personally, I hated rice. Worst invention ever. Our CO, Major Dorset, had joked that one billion Chinese couldn't be wrong. Fuck that; they were wrong. Rice sucked dick and so did Major Dorset.

Of course, the major hadn't loaded any motherfucking rice, or done anything else work related that I had ever noticed. He left that for me, Hard-on, Gordo, and the rest of Bravo Company.

The company currently consisted of two combat platoons of ten men each, a transportation unit, and for this mission, a medical corp. Normally, we fielded roughly fifty enlisted men and officers, give or take a few. Our squad leader, Specialist Tucker, was away on leave, so we were currently one man short. Bravo was a combat infantry company, so we pretty much got all the shit jobs. If there was a shitty job in a shit-hole town, in a backward-assed part of the world that needed doing, you could bet that Bravo Company would end up there doing it.

Our real job was combat, but since there wasn't always fighting to be done, we ended up doing shit jobs like loading rice into trucks... a lot.

Don't get me wrong; Ethiopia was a pretty dangerous place. Gunner and Jonesy, the other two members of our fire squad, stood guard while we worked, and Master Sergeant McAllister supervised. They had to. The local gangs liked to hijack the food deliveries. In this part of the world, food was power. Civilians couldn't work under these conditions, so the infantry had to do it. We all understood that, but it didn't keep us from bitching about it. Bitching about what you were doing was as natural as breathing in the Army. As soon as we finished loading the truck, another empty one pulled up to take its place. The hot sun beat down on us out of the bright blue, Ethiopian sky.

"Are we doing this again tomorrow, Sarge?" Hard-on groaned.

McAllister looked up from his clipboard. "You never know what tomorrow will bring, that's the best thing about being in the Army. You losers load this last truck and we'll call it a day."

We didn't know it at the time, but we had all loaded our last bag of rice.

OPS ORD 9-22

US ARMY MAJ. DORSET, CHARLES, M. AIRFIELD GRANDSTAND

EXECUTE IMMEDIATE REDEPLOYMENT OF BRAVO COMPANY TO
VILLAGE OF LAT, DEMOCRATIC REPUBLIC OF THE CONGO.
EXTRICATE MEDICAL UNIT THAT LOCATION.
DETAILS OF UNIT PERSONNEL AND MISSION TO FOLLOW.
VIRAL OUTBREAK THAT AREA, DETAILS TO FOLLOW.
IMPLEMENT SAFETY PROTOCOLS 34-7 AND 34-20.

TRANSPORT EN ROUTE YOUR LOCATION

ORDERS END

CHAPTER 3

08:33 p.m. Zulu
Air Field Grandstand
Ethiopia, Africa

The East African sun slowly sank below the horizon of the forward airbase's flight line. An incoming C-130 transport plane kicked up a swirling dust cloud that danced in the dying red light. We had a clear line of sight from our tents to the landing field. Hard-on looked up from his card hand and shaded his eyes. A second and a third C-130 followed the first plane in. The muted roar of their engines came dimly to us across the tarmac.

"That's weird," he muttered as he pushed his discards across the empty shipping crate we were using as a card table.

"Not really," I replied. I threw in my cards and took a pull on my warm beer.

"Yeah, you're right," Hard-on shot back. "I'm sure that's just our monthly shipment of strippers and crack comin' in."

Hard-on was from New Jersey and a real smart ass. He was a big guy and very muscular; he worked out with weights whenever our unit had any downtime. He considered himself a real ladies man. His real last name, Harde, had been changed to Hard-on the day he had joined the platoon. Everyone ended up with a nickname eventually. Some of them stuck, some didn't. Hard-on liked his.

"Would you two just shut up and play the game?" Jonesy complained. He pulled in the discards and shuffled the cards before dealing us all another hand. Jonesy was from Birmingham, Alabama. He had grown up in the city, and was streetwise and sharp. He was of medium build, but was very strong and fast. He had run track and wrestled in high school. Jonesy had a smooth deep voice with a strong southern drawl. If you got him drunk enough, he would sing old blues songs.

We were playing poker and drinking warm beer. Just another

Wednesday night in exotic Ethiopia. My squad played a lot of cards. Whenever we had some down time, we played Poker and Spades. Occasionally, we played for money, but Sgt. McAllister frowned on that. It caused hard feelings, so we mostly played for points, or candy and smokes.

Gunner sat on the ground nearby, idly flipping through a porno magazine. Gunner's real name was Hernandez. He was from Miami, and was mean as a snake. He had been assigned the SAW, or Squad Assault Weapon, the unit's heavy machine gun; hence his nickname, Gunner. He was short and squat, heavily tattooed, and claimed to have belonged to a gang before he joined the Army. I believed him.

"Come on, Gunner, if you get your fat ass in here we can play Euchre," Jonesy suggested.

"I hate Euchre," Gunner replied flatly.

"You ungrateful, selfish bastard," Jonesy cursed. "It doesn't matter if you like Euchre or not, *you* should play so that *we* can play. Euchre is a four person game, asshole."

Euchre was my favorite card game, but I had figured out that it was a Midwestern game; not everyone played it, or liked it for that matter. A lot of people had never heard of it. I had tried to teach it to my squad several times. Jonesy liked to play it occasionally.

"I'd rather beat my dick with a hammer than play Euchre," Gunner retorted.

"It's no wonder you're always in such a bad mood if you're masturbating with a hammer," I laughed. "You should have Hard-on show you how to do it; he's a master of self-flagellation."

Hard-on glared at me. "You should talk, Parsons, your dick looks like a pistol grip."

"If you don't like how my dick looks, stop staring at it," I suggested.

Hard-on stood up. "How'd you like a nice ass-kickin', Parsons?" he slurred. I realized we were a little too drunk for our usual game of *insult your buddy*. I had the advantage of being fairly well read and a high school diploma over my squad mates. They considered me a smart ass, and more than once I had talked myself into trouble. I had tangled with Hard-on and Gunner before. At least Jonesy had a sense of humor.

Of course, I couldn't back down, unless I did it cleverly. I slowly stood up and bowed to Hard-on.

"I apologize, Hard-on," I said seriously. "Allow me to offer a complete retraction of any slander I may have uttered about you eyeballing my junk. I'm sure you only looked in passing and it was only a harmless curiosity, perhaps gone a titch too far." I held up my finger and thumb, about an inch apart.

Hard-on was too perplexed to respond. The other two fell out laughing at the look on his face. I laughed, and finally Hard-on laughed, too. He sat back down and opened another beer.

"You're an asshole, Parsons," he muttered.

We had just settled back down to another round of poker and beers when Master Sgt. McAllister burst into our bivouac.

"Wrap this shit up, ladies," he ordered. "We are pulling out as soon as we can load up our shit."

Hard-on threw his cards in. "Damn it, Sarge! I was just starting to get drunk. I knew those planes meant trouble," he growled.

McAllister grabbed a beer, opened it, and drained it. He crushed the can and threw it at Hard-on's head. "Fun time's over. Get your kits together and hump it over to the HQ. The LT is gonna' brief everyone. The old man will be there so act straight. Got it?" he asked.

The sergeant was a good guy. He was always ripping somebody's ass, but he looked out for us. He had seen action in Iraq and Afghanistan; he knew his shit.

"Let's go!"

We cleaned ourselves up and threw on our uniform shirts and hats. It didn't take us long to pull our gear together; we were only here temporarily, and had never really completely unpacked or settled in.

The sergeant hurried us along. We walked across the base to the headquarters' tent. Usually, only the officers and senior NCOs were allowed in the tent; now, everyone was crowded inside. The tent's walls were rolled up and everyone pushed in as close as they comfortably could.

The company commander, Maj. Dorset, stood near the map board, with a pointer in hand. We called him *the old man* behind his back. Major Dorset did not engender love or loyalty in the men under his command. He was old school; like eighteenth-century British old school. He was a total prick, aloof and cold. His face was set in a constant sneer of contempt, and he rarely smiled. The major reminded me of another Army officer I had read about in my history books, General George Armstrong Custer.

He may have been fit at one time, but the major had gone soft now, and his uniforms rode a bit snug. Regardless of how the men under his command were getting on, the commander never missed a meal. He considered comfort an officer's privilege.

The old man had one golden rule: he was always correct, the reality of the situation be damned.

Standing beside him were the two combat platoon commanders, Lieutenants Reid and Beckham, the transportation NCO, Sgt. Price, and the Medical CO, Col. Warren.

Reid was competent and professional. He attempted to look after the men under his command despite the major's drawbacks. Luckily, he was our squad's commanding officer. He was tall and thin; everyone in the platoon called him the LT.

Beckham was a kiss-ass and an idiot, to boot. He was book smart, but had no experience or common sense. He just did whatever the major told him to do, and his men suffered for it. He was short, lazy, and very fat. His men had nicknamed him Fat Ass.

Everyone loved Sgt. Price. He was a big, goofy, good-natured son of a bitch. He would always help you out if he could. He smoked and drank beer and bourbon, and always made damn sure that the company was supplied with all three.

Col. Warren was a fine surgeon, and a good man to have around if you were going into a firefight. He was generally pretty friendly, but he had a serious nature. I didn't really know him, but it seemed to me that seeing men under his care die had made him melancholy.

He always seemed sad and far away.

Sgt. McAllister called everyone to attention. The old man stepped forward and snapped the pointer into his palm.

"At ease!" the major shouted. Everyone stood down and relaxed a little.

The major seemed excited. Unless we were being deployed to Tahiti, an unlikely situation at best, it probably meant more work for us.

He tried to smile and failed, and then he jumped into his speech. "Men, a situation has developed in the Democratic Republic of Congo." He moved to the map board and pointed out the DRC. "This is the village of Lat. A US Army medical unit that was dispatched there to help counter a viral outbreak has come under attack by rebel forces within the DRC. Contact has been lost with the unit. We are the closest combat company within Africa proper. We have been ordered to move to the assistance of the medical unit and to extract that unit's personnel immediately."

"I don't mean to interrupt, sir, but why are we going? Wouldn't they usually send in the Special Forces or the Rangers for a rescue mission?" Sgt. Price piped up.

"It would take at least forty-eight hours to dispatch a Special Forces unit," the major replied, "As I just explained, we are the closest combat asset."

The major looked around the tent, scowling at the men in his command. "This is a rare opportunity for all of us. Fate has given us this chance to shine, to show the world what Bravo Company can do. You will carry out this mission without fail. We will rescue the medical unit. You will make me proud. Do you understand?" the commander shouted.

"Yes, sir!" the men shouted back.

"Good," Maj. Dorset replied. "The lieutenant will brief you as to particulars, we prepare to leave immediately."

The sergeant called the men to attention again. With that, the major left the tent.

Lt. Reid stepped forward. "At ease," he said.

There was a low buzz of conversation, mostly bitching about being redeployed so quickly. The atmosphere was much more informal with the CO gone. Reid gave it a moment, and then spoke. "Listen up. I know you guys aren't happy about this. I know we just pulled three weeks of food distribution, that you guys have been busting your asses, but this mission is important. There is an American medical unit out there that needs our assistance." He paused to let that sink in. Everyone was listening now.

Hard-on piped up, "How many nurses are with that unit, sir?"

"I'm not privy to that information," Reid replied, shaking his head.

Someone shouted from the rear, "Hey, LT, did the major say something about a virus?"

"I'm glad someone was listening," the lieutenant joked. "Yes, there is a virus. We will operate in full MOPP-4 protective gear until Col. Warren clears us."

A chorus of groans broke out.

"I need you guys to hustle up. We need to have everything loaded on those C-130s and ready to go within two hours!" Reid yelled.

More groans erupted.

The LT held up his hands. "Just do it without all the bellyaching for once," he pleaded.

Sgt. McAllister stepped up and yelled, "You heard the man. Get to work! Dismissed!"

Everyone dispersed and went to work. Despite the verbal abuse, Bravo was a well-trained and efficient combat unit. Every man pitched in to help load the cargo planes.

Within two hours, our camp tents had been broken down and stowed on the transports, along with food, weapons, Humvees and a light cargo truck, all our miscellaneous combat equipment, and the medical corps' gear. Sgt. McAllister and Lt. Reid hustled back and forth between the camp and the flight line until everything was aboard.

The C-130s revved their engines as McAllister walked between them, yelling to the loaders, clipboard in hand. We stood to the side, checking and rechecking our gear. Finally, the old man boarded the lead plane. I was just glad we weren't flying with the bastard. The officers and staff flew separate from the grunts. I considered that a small blessing.

Gordo joined us; he was assigned to our squad, as we were usually on point, and had the most contact with the locals. He didn't look too happy.

"What's this I hear about wearing biological gear and gas masks?" he asked pensively. "Don't you guys know how hot it will be in the Congo? What do you know about this virus? Have you guys done this before?"

"It's standard operating procedure. Don't worry about it," I replied. "It just means that we have to wear the chem gear until the Doc checks things out. I know it sucks, but it usually doesn't take too long. The gear is hot as hell, but you kinda' get used to it after a while. Don't worry about the virus."

"Damn," Gordo replied.

I lowered my voice, "It's cool. We'll take care of you. There's ways to get around wearing the shit all the time." I winked at him.

Everything was finally loaded and strapped down. Sgt. McAllister ordered us aboard. We all trudged up the boarding ramp and took our seats on the plane. Everyone strapped in and secured their weapons and gear. The loader closed the cargo ramp door. The C-130's taxied out and took off, one by one. Our plane lifted off into the night sky and we left Ethiopia behind. We didn't have far to go.

OPS ORD 9-23

RECENT ACTIVITY BY REBEL FORCES REPORTED IN VICINITY OF LAT, DRC.

EXERCISE EXTREME CAUTION.

ORDERS END

CHAPTER 4

02:13 a.m. Zulu
Abandoned Airstrip
Democratic Republic of the Congo

Our airship sat down first on the rough grass landing strip. The pilot did his best to keep the landing smooth, but failed miserably. My body was violently rattled around against the canvas seat harness, and I clenched my teeth to keep from biting my tongue. Finally, the big plane settled down onto the poor excuse for a runway and came to a stop.

Sgt. McAllister was already up and shouting orders before the cargo door was fully open. I released the seat's safety harness and stood upright. I brought my M-4 rifle up and checked the magazine, then lowered my night vision goggles and turned them on. The plane's cargo bay turned from dim black to a bright green. I fell into line as the sergeant led us out into the tall grass.

My squad deployed along the western edge of the runway, our sister squad fanned out across the eastern side. I knelt in the tall grass and scanned the countryside around me through the NVGs. I didn't really like using the goggles if I was in a shooting situation. They limited your vision to about forty degrees directly in front of you, and you lost all of your peripheral vision. There was also no real sense of depth perception; everything looked two-dimensional and flat. For scouting work at night, they worked fine, and luckily for us, there was nothing to see here.

The second and third C-130s rolled in for their landings. As the planes shut down, they were quickly unloaded. The vehicles were pulled out and moved to one side of the field under guard. A command tent was set up, and a supply depot established.

Once everyone was offloaded, my squad was reassembled. We moved quickly around the field, setting trip wire rigged to flares in a roughly square perimeter around our assembly area.

It was noticeably warmer here than it had been on the coast. The African night was as dark as a well digger's asshole; I couldn't see shit without the NVGs. It was also a lot noisier. The damn bugs and nocturnal animals were having a screaming contest. The insects found me almost immediately, and proceeded to make me miserable. I had only been in the Congo for five minutes and I already hated it here.

Once our perimeter was secured, we moved back to the assembly area. Sgt. Price and his crew were busy loading supplies into the cargo truck and readying the Humvees.

McAllister told us to relax; we had a couple of hours before we pulled out at first light.

I found a flat piece of ground next to the vehicles and sat down. I secured my NVGs and wrapped a spare shirt around my head. I could still hear the insects, but at least it kept them out of my ears. I tried to sleep, but it was just too hot and miserable.

Finally, I got back up. I walked over to the depot tent and found some coffee. A few of the guys were grabbing some breakfast and standing around talking to the pilots. My platoon would leave at dawn, but a security team would stand by here at the airfield to protect the planes and secure the area for our return. I envied them; at least they wouldn't have to wear the chem gear.

I returned to my squad. Eventually, my exhausted body won the fight against the uncomfortable elements, and I dozed off for a couple of hours. Hard-on kicked me awake.

The sun was just coming up on the far horizon, but I could see the forest at the perimeter of the airstrip all around us. I had never seen trees that big before.

It was very warm; I was sweating already.

"The LT says to get into your suit, dick weed," Hard-on laughed evilly.

I groaned, stood up, and stretched. I pulled my MOPP-4 suit and gas mask out of my rucksack. The suit was just a pair of rubberized coveralls with tight elastic at the wrists and ankles. It had a hood that pulled over the back of the mask. I cursed through my teeth and pulled the suit over my uniform. Sweat poured from my skin. I pulled on my gas mask and adjusted the head straps. The eye lenses began to fog up immediately. Finally, I secured the hood over the mask, and drew it tight. A pair of rubber gloves completed the ensemble.

How in the world anyone expected a man to operate in Africa wearing this hot-ass clown suit was beyond me. At least we weren't marching.

The LT walked by and ordered us into the Humvee.

I clambered inside behind the others and collapsed into a jump seat. I tried not to move. It was pretty much all I could do just to breathe. The Humvee's air conditioning was a joke, but it might have been just a few precious degrees cooler inside.

The convoy pulled away from the airfield and entered the rain forest. Each squad rode in a separate Humvee, two vehicles in the front, two in the rear. The officers and medical staff were spread out among them. The cargo truck with our spare gear and supplies was in between. The point Humvee ran a short distance ahead of the convoy, just in case we hit a mine or IED. My squad followed just close enough to keep them in sight.

We were driving down a rutted dirt track through the forest. It was a very bumpy ride. Everyone was pretty tense now that we were actually in the DRC. We all knew the place was a Third World hellhole. You could run into pretty much anything out here.

Sgt. McAllister pulled his hood and mask off. His dark hair was plastered to his head with sweat. "Masks off at your own discretion," he ordered.

Everyone pulled their masks off with sighs of relief.

"I don't know how much more of that I could take," Gordo complained.

"Wait until you're out in direct sunlight," Jonesy suggested grimly.

We were only about twenty miles from the village, but the Humvees could only drive at about thirty miles an hour on the bad roads. Any faster speed would knock the teeth out of your head and risk a mechanical breakdown.

We continued down the dirt track for a good fifteen miles with no problems. I was just beginning to think we might make it to the village when suddenly our driver stood on the brakes. We slid to a shuddering stop on the track.

"Masks on!" McAllister shouted.

Everyone scrambled to pull on their masks and hoods.

The lead Humvee had stopped in the road. Its' doors opened and the crew bailed out. They took cover to either side and assumed a firing stance.

"Ah shit," McAllister cursed. "Let's get up there."

My squad scrambled out and moved up the road in pairs, two men moving forward while two covered. Sgt. McAllister and Gordo followed behind us. We stayed in the tree line to either side of the road. I reached the lead Humvee and looked around it.

Two locals were standing in the track. Both of them were dressed in battered military uniforms and armed with AK-47s. They looked like bandits or worse. I assumed we had found the rebels. One of them was a much older man, with crazy grey hair and a matted beard. He looked like an escapee from an insane asylum. He began to gesture wildly and scream at us in the local language. I couldn't understand a word of it, but he didn't sound happy. The other man had his gun at the ready, but at least no one was shooting yet.

Sgt. McAllister walked up behind me. He took in the situation at a glance and said, "I'm going forward to talk to them. Cover me."

He removed his mask and hood. He slung his rifle and stepped slowly forward into the roadway, his hands at his side.

"Gordo, lose your mask and get up here," he suggested loudly. "Everyone stand easy."

Gordo pulled off his mask and carefully walked forward. He, too, had his hands out, to show he wasn't armed.

The lead local yelled at the sergeant and pointed back the way we had come. Even I got that one.

"What the Sam Hell is he yelling about, Gordo?" the sergeant asked calmly.

Gordo frowned and listened carefully. "I'm not getting it all, Sergeant, he's pretty fucking excited. He says we must return, that we can go no further, something about the dead."

"Tell him to speak plainly, that we are stupid white men," McAllister suggested, gesturing at the dispersed squad.

Gordo spoke to the leader in broken Congolese. They got at least some of what he was saying, they both laughed and relaxed a little. The man repeated his demand.

About that time, I heard the cargo truck's engine as it approached. The major and Lt. Beckham walked up.

"What's going on here?" demanded the major.

McAllister cursed under his breath. "We're trying to figure it out, sir. I've got it under control."

The man pointed at the major and jerked his finger, then yelled his warning again.

"Why are these two Kaffirs holding up my convoy? Give these men some cigarettes or whiskey and let's get this convoy moving again, Sergeant!" the major ordered. "We don't have time for this!"

Gordo spoke up, "They don't want anything, Major. This man is trying to warn us."

"Well, what is he saying?" the major demanded.

The man yelled again. He seemed to be growing agitated.

"He says that we must go no further, that the people before us will be turned against us, that we will find the dead, no, our death, wait, something about we cannot return," Gordo translated.

"Fuck this; we need to get to the village, now. There are only two of them," the major growled.

"Wait!" Sgt. McAllister warned. "Sir, don't do anything stupid. There are armed men in the trees to either side of us."

"We are a US Army combat company on a lawful rescue mission," Major Dorset snapped. "I will not be delayed by a handful of ragtag rebels. Tell that man to step aside or we will open fire," the major growled.

The major's tone was not lost on the rebels. The leader yelled his warning again, and the man beside him jerked up his rifle.

Everyone tensed to fire.

McAllister spoke loudly but in a calm voice, "Hold your fire." He punctuated each word.

"Tell him!" the major barked.

Gordo repeated the major's demand to the rebel leader. The man seemed to be gauging the American's resolve. He looked around at the platoon and back down the track. Second Platoon was slowly advancing to cover us. His eyes narrowed. He slowly reached out and forced his companion's rifle barrel down. They turned and walked away, disappearing into the trees.

"That is how you deal with the locals, Sergeant!" the major smirked. He noticed that the sergeant and Gordo weren't wearing their masks. "Why have you disobeyed my order to wear protective gear at all times?"

Sgt. McAllister shook his head. "I was trying to secure our passage, sir. I felt it necessary to remove my mask to speak with the locals."

"No one is to remove their MOPP-4 protective equipment for any reason!" the major yelled. "Report to me once we are established in the village, Sergeant," he rumbled.

"Yes, sir!" the sergeant replied, yanking his gas mask back on and drawing his hood. He turned and stalked away.

"Move out!" the CO ordered.

We remounted and drove onward through the trees. Ten minutes later, we reached the village of Lat.

TO THE JOINT CHIEFS OF STAFF – CODE RED COMMUNIQUE

UNABLE TO REESTABLISH CONTACT WITH MEDICAL UNIT LAT DRC

CIA ANALYSIS CONFIRMS SPREAD OF VIRUS THROUGHOUT IMMEDIATE REGION

BRAVO COMPANY IN ROUTE

SPECIAL FORCES UNIT ACTIVATED

REPORT ENDS

CHAPTER 5

08:35 a.m. Zulu
Village of Lat
The Congo

We stopped and dismounted at the edge of the village, as soon as we cleared the tree line. I could tell something was wrong the minute we arrived. You develop a sixth sense about things after you've been in combat, and you learn to trust that instinct. It keeps you alive.

The village felt like an ambush to me.

There wasn't much to see. The rutted jungle road petered out into a muddy patch of puddles and stones. A few dozen slat-board huts with corrugated metal roofs surrounded a small, beat-up-looking church. The obligatory cinder block clinic and a couple of more modern-looking buildings with metal siding comprised the village center. The whole place was carved out of the surrounding rain forest. The massive trees pressed in from all sides. Their twisting, exposed roots thrust through the mud like loops of blackened mooring cables. Here and there, I could see a few pathetic scratch gardens filled with scraggly, drooping vegetables. I didn't see any people. Of course, they could be in hiding, but I didn't like the vibe.

The medical unit personnel we had been sent in to rescue were nowhere in sight. No one came out to meet us. Their tents and vehicles were set up to one side of the village, on our right. Everything there was in disarray. Two of the smaller tents were partially collapsed, and one of their Humvee's windshields was smashed. Debris of all sorts littered the ground. It didn't look good, but I didn't see any bodies.

Maj. Dorset walked forward and looked around. "Let's find our people," he ordered.

McAllister sprang into action. "You heard the man!" he shouted. "1st Platoon, secure the village. 2nd Platoon, with the major. Let's look for our people." He pointed towards the tents.

I was with 1st Platoon. The platoon split into two squads and advanced. We spread out and moved slowly forward into the village. I stalked through the muddy lane, my M-4 rifle at the ready. Once again, we moved in advance and cover formation, two moving, two covering. There were footprints everywhere, and in at least two places, I found congealed pools of blood. I stooped down and traced a set of military boot prints in the mud. They led deeper into the maze of huts. I pointed them out to Hard-on. He grunted in reply.

We cleared each hut as we came to them. Each was the same. They were all empty.

We approached the church. All of us stopped to stare. Gummy, blackened bloodstains covered the chapel's walls and floors. The front steps were a mass of bloody footprints and splattered gore.

"What have we gotten into?" Jonesy spoke.

"This is some Old Testament shit right here, boys," Hard-on uttered.

"It is bad, very bad," Gunner warned. He crossed himself.

I wasn't really what you would consider overtly religious, but seeing that bloodstained chapel sent shivers down my spine. Hard-on was right.

"How many people had to die to make that much blood?" Jonesy asked.

"A lot," I answered.

One of the buildings was what passed for a store. We cautiously stepped inside. The place was messy, and we found faint bloodstains, but it had not been looted. Some of the foodstuffs and supplies had been knocked from the shelves, but that was all.

Hard-on stepped behind the tiny counter and rummaged around. He held up a handful of the local currency.

"This ain't normal for Africa, boys," Jonesy pointed out.

We cleared the other small building; it was a residence of some sort, just a little nicer than the huts around it. It was the same.

Nobody was home.

We moved forward again, very carefully, and cleared the village, hut by empty hut.

"Where the fuck is everybody?" Gunner asked.

"Who knows?" I replied.

"I don't like this," Gunner spat back. "Something seriously wrong went down here."

I knew what he meant. Death had touched this place. The sweat ran cold under my chem suit.

Jonesy and Gunner moved forward. We had cleared the village and reached the end. The rain forest stretched out before us, a solid wall of trees, grim, green and foreboding on the other side.

We turned around and made our way back.

Everyone rendezvoused at the medical unit's camp. Sgt. McAllister came out to meet us.

"Well?" he asked.

"Nothing, Sarge. There's nobody out there," I reported. "No bodies, none of our personnel, not a damn thing. The village is empty. We did find blood, a lot of blood."

I told him about the chapel.

"I'll have to look at that. Anything else unusual?" he asked.

"Nothing was looted!" Hard-on added. "Everything is still there."

The sergeant grunted in response. "Wait till you boys see this."

He led us through the medical unit's camp and stopped at one of the damaged tents.

"We didn't find any of our people either, but we did find human remains. The colonel is trying to ascertain if the remains belonged to us, or the villagers. It's hard to tell."

"What do you mean, Sarge?" Jonesy asked.

"The remains had been eaten, chewed, whatever. Fucking Africa. Must have been scavengers, hyenas maybe. There wasn't much left that was identifiable. The bugs and flies had been at them pretty hard. Looks like it had been a day or more. We found a lot of blood, too. It's everywhere."

"Sweet Jes…" Hard-on started.

"Don't blaspheme!" Gunner shouted. "This place is cursed! Don't take the Lord's name in vain here, it's bad enough already!"

"Knock it off, you two," McAllister growled. "Look here."

He pointed to the ground around the tent. Hundreds of spent shell casings littered the ground. He picked a couple out of the mud and tossed them in his calloused hand. "Standard NATO 556x45 and nine-millimeter, government issue. There was a pretty sharp firefight here. Somebody was shooting with an M-4 and a Beretta. We found a couple of rifles near this tent, they had been fired recently, one had blood on it. Our guys didn't go out without a fight."

Every good soldier learned to interpret the evidence left on a battleground. Sgt. McAllister was an expert at it.

"What about the other tents?" I asked.

"They were empty, everything was a total mess," the sergeant replied. "I haven't been past the biological seals in the clean tent. The colonel went in there. He hasn't come out yet, but he ordered it sealed."

"What do you think happened here, Sergeant?" Hard-on asked.

"Your guess is as good as mine," he replied. "In all my years of soldiering, I've never seen anything like this. You guys stay close, I'm going to talk to the old man and see what our next move is."

McAllister ducked into the command tent. We wandered around the area, but there wasn't much else to see. The medical guys were clearing the area, putting the camp back in order. Sgt. Price and a couple of the transport grunts were looking over the damaged Humvee. We walked over to talk to him.

"What happened to her?" I asked.

"Some asshole broke out the windshield," Price answered, "And they sprung the driver's door, it's damned near pulled off." He cursed. "This is gonna' set the taxpayers back a pretty penny. I figure there's four or five thousand dollars-worth of damage."

"Yeah, but how did it happen?" I queried.

"I don't fucking know. I just fix 'em up after you assholes trash 'em," Price laughed.

Sgt. McAllister came to collect us.

"The major wants me to send out 1st Platoon to look for survivors," he said.

"We already looked for them," Hard-on complained.

"The major wants you to search the forest surrounding the village," McAllister explained. "I tried to talk him out of it, but he insists. He wants all of the medical unit's personnel accounted for. I need you guys to do a sweep of the area around the village."

"Shit, Sarge," Hard-on grumbled.

"Just do it," McAllister shot back. "I want you guys on red. There could be rebels out there. Stay sharp. Stay together and stay close to the village, I don't need you fuckers getting lost on top of everything else. I've got enough on my plate already."

1st Platoon saddled up and moved into the forest. We started on the side nearest our camp. We flipped a coin to see which squad would move the furthest into the forest. My squad lost, of course. The sun was up and it was hot, even under the canopy of the trees. We all bitched and cursed and cussed, but we followed orders.

Walking slowly in our pressure cooker suits, we spread out and searched the forest. We established a line formation, so that each man could see the men next to him on either side. The lenses of my gas mask kept fogging up, and the green gloom of the woods made it hard to see. I felt like my eyes were playing tricks on me. I would see movement ahead of me through the trees, but there was nothing there once we carefully advanced.

We moved gradually forward, winding our way through the giant tree trunks, creepers, and ferns. Our sight was sometimes limited to a few yards; we struggled to maintain contact with each other. We had only searched for a short time before Gunner called out to us.

I pushed through the foliage to his position; the others were already there. Gunner was kneeling on the loam. He used his bayonet to lift a bloodstained, heavily rent shirt from the mud. It was mangled and dirty, but bits of green peeked through the stains.

"It's a scrub," Gunner whispered. "It was one of ours."

We all stared at the dangling shirt. I tried to get my head around how it could have been damaged that badly. It looked like its previous owner had been run through a wood chipper.

"I wonder what happened to the guy who was wearing it?" Jonesy muttered.

"Nothing good," I replied. "Bring that along, Gunner. Let's keep on looking."

We resumed our search formation and pushed on through the forest. A little further on, we crossed a trail and entered a small, overgrown glade. The remains of a badly corroded truck and an ancient backhoe lay rusting in the mud. They looked like they had been abandoned for a decade or more. A few tree stumps dotted the clearing, but nature had made short work of man's progress, and the rain forest was quickly reclaiming the spot. These were common-place to us. Africa was a vast graveyard of abandoned equipment and failed ventures.

We continued on with our circuit. I wasn't sure how far around the village we had come, but we were turning to our left. The man closest to the village was supposed to keep it in his sight. Jonesy and I were the two men furthest out. Jonesy had drifted away until I could barely see him through the trees.

I heard him yell. I stopped and shouted to everyone further down the line. My squad stopped and moved towards us.

I struggled over to Jonesy; he was pointing further into the forest.

"Guys! I've got a survivor!" Jonesy yelled. "It's one of ours!"

We all moved forward. Jonesy pointed into the trees. I could see someone emerging from the forest. I lowered my gun; it was a nurse in mud-splattered, torn green scrubs. She staggered forward and stopped. Her face was a swollen mass of bruises, and dried blood covered her tattered clothing. Patches of pale flesh showed through the rents in her scrubs. She was obviously wounded and in shock.

"Hey!" Jonesy yelled. He slung his rifle and walked to her.

She took a few faltering steps towards him and lifted her arms.

"Get a medic!" Jonesy yelled. "She's hurt bad!"

Jonesy took the nurse by her arm. She turned and grappled with him. Her teeth sank into his shoulder, tearing through his chem suit like tissue paper. Jonesy's screams were muffled by his gas mask. Blood spurted as they went down in a tangle of flailing limbs.

"What the fuck?" Hard-on yelled. He leaped forward and grabbed the struggling nurse by her neck. He punched her in the head and flung her roughly aside.

Jonesy struggled upright, one hand clamped to his lacerated shoulder. Blood ran freely through his fingers. "She fucking bit me!" he shrieked.

The nurse slowly sat upright and began to crawl back towards Jonesy. A bloodcurdling moan came through her mangled lips. Her face was a snarling mask of blood.

Without conscious thought, I lifted my gun and fired. It was my soldier's instinct that took over, reacting to a threat close at hand. I was only two yards from the nurse. I couldn't miss. A three shot burst took her through the chest. The heavy rounds blew off her left breast and shattered her arm. She was thrown backwards into the mud.

Hard-on took two steps towards me. He knocked my gun aside and roughly pushed me back.

"Why are you shooting, Parsons?" he screamed into my face.

"She attacked Jonesy!" I yelled back. "Fuck's sake, man. Look at her!"

"Guys!" Gunner shouted. We turned to look at him. He was pointing to the nurse.

She slowly sat up and struggled to her feet, pushing herself up from the mud with her one good arm. I could see into her ribcage... her heart was gone, her vitals were shredded. She couldn't possibly still be alive. She took three faltering steps towards us.

Gunner screamed and opened up with the SAW. The gun roared and the nurse disintegrated into flopping chunks of bloody black meat. Her severed upper torso and head slapped down into the mud.

"Fuck me," Hard-on stuttered, backing away. I could hear him retching inside his suit.

What was left of the nurse was attempting to crawl towards us. The bloody arm extended and the hand grasped, clawing for purchase in the mud. The thing's bloodshot eyes bulged, and its teeth snapped.

We all stared at the struggling monstrosity in utter disbelief.

No one gave the command to fire; we all emptied our guns until only a severed hand remained. It flopped in the mud like a fish.

"What the hell is going on, man?" Gunner demanded shakily. "What was that thing?" He made the sign of the cross and hastily reloaded the SAW.

Hard-on stepped forward. He cursed and stomped on the hand until it was buried under the mud, out of our sight.

I helped Jonesy to his feet. He was still bleeding heavily. I remembered the virus.

"Come on!" I shouted, pulling Jonesy along. "We have to get Jonesy back to the medics."

We pulled back towards the village, cutting through the woods towards our camp.

"The shit is gonna' hit the fan when they find out we wasted that nurse," Hard-on cursed.

We reached the village. The other squad had stopped there to wait for us. Their squad leader, Specialist Sadler, came over to meet us.

"What the fuck is going on?" he demanded. "What were you shooting at?"

"We don't fucking know!" Hard-on growled.

I helped Jonesy over to them.

"What happened?" Sadler inquired. "Did he get shot?"

"No, he got bit," I responded.

"Bit?" Sadler repeated.

"That's what the man said," Hard-on confirmed. "This fucking bitch came out of the woods a ways out there. When we tried to help her, she bit him."

"A local?" Sadler asked.

"No, she was one of ours," I replied.

31

"Where is she?" Sadler inquired.

"We wasted her; we wasted her hard," Gunner answered. "There was something wrong with her. She was possessed by the devil."

"You assholes shot a survivor?" Sadler asked incredulously.

"Yeah, well you weren't there. I told you, she attacked Jonesy. She was trying to kill him!" I replied.

Sadler shook his head in disbelief, "Let's get him back to camp. The LT can sort this shit out."

We helped Jonesy back to our camp. Two of the medical corpsmen came and took him into one of the tents. As we limped in, Sgt. McAllister came out to meet us.

"Report!" he barked. "Who was shooting out there?"

I quickly told him what had happened. He didn't seem happy at all.

"Sadler, Parsons, go inside and debrief the old man," he ordered. "I'll try to do what I can for you. The rest of you give 2nd Platoon a hand."

Sadler looked at me. I shrugged and walked to the command tent. Sgt. McAllister went with us.

We ducked inside. The first area inside was just a normal tent. Two tables and a map board were set up, along with a communications array. A sealed flap against the far wall led further inside. Beyond it was a decontamination area, and then the clean tent. I had experienced all of this before from dozens of drills and exercises.

The CO and the lieutenants were seated at the first table; they looked up as we entered.

I assumed they knew that shots had been fired.

Sadler didn't move so I stepped forward.

"Did you find any of our personnel?" the major asked.

"Yes, sir," I answered. I related our encounter with the nurse and how she had attacked Jonesy. Sadler confirmed that Jonesy had been wounded.

"Am I to understand that you opened fire on an unarmed nurse, one of the personnel we were sent here to rescue?" the major barked. "And that she is now dead?"

"Yes, sir," I replied. I had learned long ago that it was better to keep your answers short and sweet. The more you talked, the deeper you got yourself into the shit with the old man. You couldn't get a word in anyway until he had ripped your ass for a while and he ran out of steam.

"She must have been infected with the virus, sir," Lt. Reid spoke up in my defense.

"No doubt," the major replied dryly. "Parsons, I should have you taken outside and shot!" He rose in a fury and shouted at me. I could actually see the spittle hitting the inside of his mask. "It is within my powers as a field commander to do so!"

"Sir, I must protest!" the sergeant yelled, coming to attention.

"Be still, Sgt. McAllister!" the major roared. "This man has shot a non-combatant. More importantly to me, he has shot one of the personnel I was ordered to rescue!"

The major came even closer to me. I could see the veins in his bloodshot eyes.

"Do you think I like being in Africa, Parsons?" he barked, lowering his voice just a little. "Do you think I enjoy leading this pathetic excuse for a command around on peace-keeping missions and food-distribution outings for the poor, starving, abandoned children of ignorant, backwards people who are too dumb to figure out how to use a condom?"

His voice rose with each word until he was at full boil. "We had a simple mission to do here. All we had to do was roll in and rescue a single, stupid medical unit from the stinking local rebels. Come here, rescue our personnel, and leave!"

He stopped screaming for a moment and sank back into his chair. I didn't dare utter a word. I just stood at attention and didn't move.

No one spoke for a moment.

Finally, the old man started back up again, "This was my ticket out of here. I could have gone back to the States, or Europe, anywhere but Africa. This place is a fucking shit-hole. Everything here is covered in flies and shit. I fucking hate it here. Do you understand what you've done to me, Parsons? You've fucked me!

You had better work real hard to die here because as soon as we get back to the real world, I'm gonna bring you up on charges and throw your ass in the brig. You're going to Leavenworth, you worthless fucker! I'm going to make it my life's work to make sure you rot there!"

The major finally ran out of steam. I was a little concerned, he seemed fairly mad.

No one spoke for a long moment. We weren't sure if he was quite finished or not.

Finally, Sgt. McAllister spoke up, "Are we dismissed, sir?"

"Not quite," the major replied. "I want Parson's squad to retrieve the nurse's body. At the least we can make sure her remains are returned to her family. In the future, endeavor to not shoot any more of our people, Specialist Parsons," he ordered. "I want them brought back alive."

"She wasn't alive, sir," I risked replying.

"Nonsense," the major retorted. "I'm not buying into your story. It is obvious to me that you panicked. Everyone here before our arrival seems to have contracted the virus. They are sick, possibly deranged, but they are very much alive. Let's keep the rest of them that way, shall we? Dismissed! Get the fuck out of my sight!"

We came to attention and ducked back outside.

Sgt. McAllister took me by the arm, and steered me off to one side. "You need to stay clear of the old man, I mean like for the rest of this trip," he warned me. "I know you prefer to make light of your ass-chewings, but he's not fucking around this time. He wants to put you away."

"Yeah, maybe you're right," I concurred.

"Damn straight I'm right," he said. "Lay low, and don't fuck up again. I can only cover so much of your ass, boy."

I went by the medical unit's supply tent and grabbed a body bag. No one asked me why I needed it.

I found the rest of my squad and filled them in on what had been said.

Hard-on laughed, "Man, I am so glad the old man singled you out."

"Lucky you," I retorted. "I took the heat. You're welcome, motherfuckers!"

"Hey, you shot first. We just jumped in to help you out," Hard-on countered.

"You were right to shoot," Gunner spoke up. "That woman, she was possessed."

"That's bullshit!" Hard-on opined. "That bitch was sick with the virus, she was out of her gourd, bat-shit crazy, that's all."

"You're both wrong," I stated. "You fuckers saw her. Her heart was blown out of her chest and she got up and came at us again. Explain that shit to me."

"Your body can run on adrenaline for a minute or so after your heart stops beating, that's a proven fact," Hard-on answered.

"Not when you take three rounds, point blank. You don't get back up from that. The shock alone will kill you stone dead. And what about when just her fucking head and an arm tried to attack us, huh? What about that?" I concluded.

Gunner shuddered and crossed himself three times, "Demonic possession."

"Bullshit," Hard-on grunted. "What do you think it is, smart ass?" he asked me.

"I'll tell you what's going on," I answered him. "There is only one possibility that explains everything we've seen here. That fucking virus is reanimating the people it kills. It's turning them into zombies."

We all agreed to disagree.

We carefully made our way back through the forest to the spot where we had encountered the nurse. It was even hotter now; we were all melting like giant sticks of stinky butter inside our chem suits.

The flies helped us locate her again. I held open the bag while the other two pushed what was left of her into it with sticks. It wasn't pretty. I had to try hard not to puke into my mask.

"Should we dig up her hand?" Gunner asked.

"Fuck that man, we got enough of her, let's go!" Hard-on barked.

I was too disgusted to argue. I got to carry the bag by a two-to-one vote. It wasn't really that heavy.

We staggered back to the tents and turned over her remains to a nauseated corpsman.

Since we were already there, we checked on Jonesy. They couldn't tell us anything other than that he was sick, presumably with the virus. I was just glad to hear that he was still alive.

We tried to find some place out of the sun to sit down for a while. We had just appropriated a spot under a supply area tarp and broke out the cards when the LT came and found us.

"Nice work back there, Parsons," he complained. "You got my ass in a sling too."

"Sorry, LT," I offered.

"Whatever, the CO is pissed. He wants you and your squad out in the boonies until all the medical personnel are accounted for," the LT replied.

"Come on, LT," Hard-on moaned. "We just came in. We're dying out there in this chem gear!"

"Hey, you guys brought this on yourselves," Reid countered. "Take off. And don't come back without the missing personnel. And don't shoot anymore of them, Parsons!"

We painfully walked back into the forest. The other two were angry, and wouldn't talk to me. I didn't give a shit; they were hardly sparkling conversationalists.

I was on point; Hard-on took the right, Gunner the left. We circled the village, and, finding nothing, started to circle it back. It was so fucking hot that we could barely walk.

We had just stopped at an intersection where two faint trails came together, leading back towards the village behind us. Both of them ran away into the forest. You couldn't see more than fifty yards down either one.

I was trying to get some water out of my canteen and through the stupid straw past my gas mask when Gunner grabbed my arm.

"Look," he hissed. He pointed down the trail to our right. A man was slowly limping up the trail towards our position.

"Dude, he is all fucked up!" Hard-on whispered.

Fucked up was a strong understatement. The man was a walking piece of pepperoni pizza. His skin was gone, literally peeled or chewed away. You could clearly see his musculature and the bone of his skull. He had been skinned alive.

"The Saints save us," Gunner whispered fiercely. "His face, and his eyes. They're gone!"

"Ah, shit," I responded.

"What?" Hard-on urged.

"He's wearing scrubs."

I didn't think the man could hear us; he didn't have any ears. Still, just to be safe we slowly backed away from him, and held a hurried, whispered conference off the trail.

"We have to take him back," I urged.

"Are you fucking kidding me, man?" Hard-on asked. "That guy has definitely got the virus. There is no way he should still be walkin' around. I am not touching that fucker! No way."

"So you agree with me now, that he is definitely dead, right?" I asked.

"No, asshole, I don't. I think that poor bastard is so sick that he doesn't realize he's been skinned alive," Hard-on retorted.

"Come on," I groaned. "I guarantee you that prick does not have a pulse!"

"Dead men can't walk!" Hard-on hissed.

The man was slowly moving closer to us, but I didn't think he had spotted us yet.

Gunner was as nervous as a long-tailed cat in a room full of rocking chairs. It was all he could do not to run away.

"Gunner, take it easy man," I urged.

"That is not a man," he insisted. "That is a demon."

It was hard to tell, but the man was still wearing the remains of a tattered pair of green scrubs. The shirt was almost completely gone, but the pants were mostly intact, just heavily bloodstained. I pointed them out to my companions.

"Demons don't wear pants," I stated. "And that guy is one of the pricks we are looking for. If we ever want to get back on the old man's good side, we have to take him back!"

"Shit!" Hard-on hissed.

I wasn't happy about it either, especially with these two assholes helping me. Hard-on didn't want to go near the thing, and Gunner was completely terrified of it.

I looked at my rifle and cursed. We couldn't just shoot it. I desperately tried to come up with a plan, but I was drawing a blank.

Finally, I just decided to tackle it from behind.

Hard-on and I pulled back off the trail as quietly as we could, on opposite sides. Once we were in position, Gunner stood up and waved his arms. He yelled curses in Spanish and English at the thing on the path. I guess the thing heard him, because it jerked its grotesque head up and staggered towards him. Gunner didn't wait as long as I would have liked. He turned and ran back towards the village.

The thing stumped along the path as quickly as it could, dragging one crippled foot behind it. It moved past us without slowing down. Seeing it up close did not help to steel my resolve to capture it. Hundreds of hungry flies swarmed around it in a droning cloud. I could actually hear them through my hood. Seeing the thing turned my stomach; I had to keep telling myself it was once a man. It moaned pitifully through its mangled mouth.

It hobbled past me, and I forced myself to crawl forward onto the trail. I gave it a few seconds to move away. It didn't look back. I hoped Hard-on was up for this shit.

I silently rose and sprinted down the trail. I threw myself forward in a flying tackle, hitting the thing high in the shoulders, and pinning its arms to the sides. We went down hard in the mud, sliding forward on the trail. I wrapped up the creature with my legs and held on for dear life. A horrible rotten stench came through my gas mask, strongly enough to make my eyes water. I gasped for air and retched. The thing thrashed violently underneath me, twisting its gory head from side to side, attempting to bite me. Its moans turned to growls. We wrestled in the mud. I was not a happy camper.

"Hard-on, you worthless fucker, get up here now!" I screamed in my highest falsetto, each word rising higher to a terrified shriek. It was all I could do to hang on.

Hard-on bent down until he could see my face. He was a good ten feet away.

"What do I do now?" he asked.

"Get over here, you fuck!" I screamed. "Get something in this fucker's mouth before he bites me!"

My grasp wasn't holding. The damn thing was slippery and determined to get me. I was holding onto a man made out of slimy, rotted meat.

"What do I do?" Hard-on demanded.

"Use your rifle's sling!" I shouted back. "Hurry!"

Hard-on unclipped his M-4's sling and crept timidly forward.

"Do it!" I howled.

Hard-on carefully draped the sling over the man's jerking, snapping head, and pulled it into its mouth. The thing immediately clamped onto the sling's padding. Hard-on drew the webbing tight through the adjustment clip. He leapt back.

I was still struggling to hold on.

"What now?" Hard-on asked.

Gunner had finally crept back to us; he stood looking fearfully down at the trashing monstrosity.

"Get Gunner's strap!" I suggested.

It wasn't bad enough that I had to wrestle with a struggling, virus-laden dead guy; I also had to shout directions to these two brain-dead dickheads.

Hard-on grabbed Gunner's sling. He wrapped it repeatedly around the thing's feet and tied it off. I shifted my hold and sat upright. Now I was just holding the thing's arms down.

"You'll have to help me with this part," I grunted. "Gunner, get the sling off my rifle."

Gunner moved back up the trail and retrieved my M-4. He

unclipped the sling and threw it to Hard-on.

"I'm going to pull his hands together, wrap 'em up real tight," I panted.

I slowly forced the man's hands together behind his back and lifted them as high as I could. Hard-on finally grew a set of balls. He wrapped the thing's wrists together and pulled the strap so tight that it sank into the meat. He tied the strap off and stepped back to admire his work.

With a groan, I released the struggling, moaning, hogtied creature and rolled to the side. I painfully got upright and stood bent over, gasping for breath in the trail.

"Do you guys think you could have helped me any slower?" I growled.

"It was your bright idea to catch this fucker," Hard-on replied. "Why didn't we bring some duct-tape or something?"

"I didn't actually think we would find anybody!" I shot back.

Hard-on knelt down beside our captive and looked him over. He waved his hand back and forth. "Man, this guy stinks!"

The creature thrashed and groaned.

"Hey, he's pretty active for a dead guy," Hard-on observed. "You still think he's a zombie?"

"I don't know," I replied. I wasn't sure how to tell. I couldn't tell if he was breathing, and I couldn't take his pulse with gloves on. I shrugged and shook my head.

Gunner had moved away from us, I could hear him quietly praying.

I looked down at my suit. It was covered in slime and mud, but it didn't appear to be ripped or damaged. I figured I would probably be okay, but I smelled like rotten ass.

"Let's get this cocksucker back to camp," I suggested. "Maybe then they'll believe us."

We cut a stout sapling down and thrust it through our captive's arms, behind his back. Hard-on took one end and I took the other. We lifted the trashing, bloody red bastard and slowly pulled him through the forest. Gunner took point and led us back, pausing occasionally to let us catch up.

We had to stop and rest several times, but we finally made it back to our camp.

Everyone turned out to see the bloody monster we had hauled in out of the woods. Major Dorset took one look at it and ordered the corpsmen to take it away, out of sight. According to him, it was bad for morale. They pulled the struggling body into a tent and closed the flaps tight. You could still dimly hear its moans.

The colonel came out of the clean tent and went in after it. He didn't come back out.

Everyone stood around in small groups, talking in hushed tones and whispers.

"The show is over!" the major finally shouted. "Everyone get back to work!" He looked at me with murder in his eyes, but he had ordered us to bring the thing back.

Sgt. McAllister led me and the others away from the HQ.

"Go through decontamination, all of you," he ordered.

We trudged over to the decontamination area, and stood with our arms outstretched. A corpsman sprayed us down with hot soapy water and an anti-viral foam, while another one scrubbed us with a long poled brush. Finally, they hit us with water again and turned us loose. We staggered back towards camp.

McAllister was waiting for us.

"You three are something else," he laughed.

"What?" I asked.

"The safest place for you right now is out there in the forest, and you three assholes wander back in here with the elephant man in tow. The major is madder than all Hell."

"Well, we were followin' his orders," Hard-on quipped.

"Don't be so fucking dense, Hard-on," Sarge replied. "I don't think the old man thought you would find anything like that monstrosity you guys dredged up. But since you did, we're going back out to look for more!"

"What?" Gunner groaned.

"Yes, sir," the sergeant drawled. "You three are to head back out to wherever you found that guy and see what else you can dig up. I'm taking Gordo with me, way, way out there, to see what's going on. Maybe we can find some locals to talk to."

"Shit," Hard-on moaned. "When will this crap end?"

"Don't know," McAllister answered. "But the colonel wants us to find him one of the missing villagers too. He wants to see if the virus is doing the same thing to them that it is doing to us. Our orders are to acquire an infected villager and bring him back to the HQ. I volunteered your squad for the job, seeing as how you've got the most experience with the virus' victims."

"Thanks," I muttered.

"You're welcome," he replied. "Get your asses back in the brush."

"We need to find some duct tape first," Hard-on joked.

We walked through the forest a short distance away from the camp. I was so hot and tired that I could barely walk. The wet pants legs of my uniform were chaffing my inner thighs, and my feet were squishing inside my boots.

"Let's just find a place to hide for a while, and get some fucking rest," Hard-on suggested.

"I'm not walkin' around no more," Gunner agreed.

"Cool by me," I said. "I don't think I can get in any more trouble than I'm already in."

We found a tightly packed clump of smaller trees and squeezed inside the tiny clearing between them. Each of us claimed a trunk to lean back against. I sank down on my ass with my rifle across my knees and gratefully closed my eyes.

We probably should have set a guard.

REPORT FROM COLONEL WARREN, MEDICAL CO BRAVO

COMPUTER RECORDS AND INITIAL ANALYSIS DATA FROM
COLONEL ORTEGA'S UNIT RECOVERED. TO BE FORWARDED
AS ANALYZED. CANNOT CONFIRM ORTEGA'S HYPOTHESIS
WITHOUT CULTURES.

ALL MEDICAL PERSONNEL MISSING ASSUMED KIA. SOME
HUMAN REMAINS RECOVERED, STILL UNIDENTIFIED.

BODY OF SPECIALIST THOMAS BRADFORD RECOVERED.
BRADFORD TESTS POSITIVE FOR UNIDENTIFIED VIRUS
AND   SUFFERED   SEVERE   DAMAGE,   POSSIBLE
CANNIBALIZATION?

VIRUS CAUSES EXTREME MODIFICATIONS TO HUMAN
PHYSIOLOGY, CANNOT FORWARD DETAILS WITHOUT
FURTHER
VERIFICATION OF ANALYSIS.

TRANSMISSION ENDS
COLONEL WARREN, US ARMY MEDICAL CORP

CHAPTER 6

12:02 p.m. Zulu
The Congo
Africa

I'm not sure how long I was out, but something woke me up just in time. I heard a low moaning noise dimly through my mask and hood. I rubbed the lenses of my gas mask to clear them. Something was reaching for me through the trees.

One of the infected villagers was grasping for me with one outstretched arm. I was mere inches from his struggling, blackened fingertips. The man had wedged his bloated belly between two of the tree trunks we had climbed over to get into our hiding place. Gunner and Hard-on were still out cold.

I kicked them awake.

Gunner practically climbed his tree, screaming in Spanish. Hard-on didn't panic quite as badly, but he wasn't too happy either. I moved away from the thing as far as I could.

We all watched the man struggle to reach us. If a skinny villager had found us, we would have been fucked. This guy wasn't as bad as the pepperoni man, but he wasn't going to win any beauty contests either. He had several nasty wounds on his arms, shoulders, neck, and face. They were all crusted with dried black blood. I pointed out that they all looked suspiciously like bite marks. His eyes were a nasty, filmed-over yellow color; they looked like a dead man's eyes. Every soldier who had ever killed a man knew those eyes. He had collected a few hundred flies of his own. We couldn't smell him through the masks, but I was willing to bet he smelled bad; dipped in shit, three days dead, stinky, triple fucked, Ugandan whorehouse pussy bad.

"This shit's getting way out of hand," Hard-on observed once he calmed down enough to speak coherently.

I talked Gunner down and we discussed what to do.

"Let's get the fuck gone out of here, before it gets loose," Gunner suggested.

"Now, wait a minute," I said thoughtfully. "We should take this fucker back to camp."

"No, that is a very bad idea," Gunner replied.

"No, it is a good idea, and let me tell you why," I began. "If we turn this poor bastard over to the colonel, maybe he'll finally figure out what's going on out here. Maybe he'll find an antidote. Hell, maybe he'll pull his head out of his ass and realize that the people we were sent here to save are all dead, and then we can get the fuck outta' here!"

"I don't know," Hard-on said slowly.

"This one will be easy," I pointed out. "He's already half way in the bag."

They finally agreed to help me.

Gunner kept his attention while Hard-on and I climbed out of the trees on the other side of the grove. It looked clear, so we crept around to the struggling villager's ass end. I held his feet together while Hard-on wrapped his ankles in duct tape. I climbed up on top of him and used the rifle sling trick to secure his mouth; it worked like a charm. Finally, we climbed back into the grove and poked at him with a stick. When he grabbed it, we quickly wound his wrists together with the tape. Took us all of five minutes to wrap him up.

Hard-on and I grabbed the waistband of his pants and hauled him out of the trees. We dumped him on his face in the mud. He struggled to stand up. I put a boot to his ass and then stood on him.

"We need another pole," I suggested.

We struggled into camp with our prize, but this time, only a couple of corpsmen came out to meet us. They removed the pole and pushed him onto a stretcher. They secured him with bungee cords and picked him up.

"Where are you taking him?" I asked

"He's going into the sample tent with the others," he replied.

"The sample tent?" Hard-on asked.

"That is what the colonel calls it," the corpsman answered. "All of the specimens you guys have brought in are in there. Don't ask me what the colonel is doing with them. You don't want to know."

They carried the struggling, groaning villager away and disappeared into one of the larger tents.

I noticed a constant, muffled moaning. It was coming from the tent they had gone into.

"Do you guys hear that?" I inquired.

"It sounds like a dozen of those things," Hard-on responded.

"This place is cursed; it is a place of the damned." Gunner swore. "Let's go away from here."

"We need to find the Sarge," I suggested.

We wandered around the camp, asking for Sgt. McAllister. We finally found him at the decontamination area. Some of 2nd Platoon's guys were there being processed.

"I wondered where you guys got off to," McAllister said.

"Did you and Gordo find anything?" I inquired.

"Yeah, we brought in another medic, he wasn't as bad as the one you guys bagged," the sergeant answered.

"We found another one, Sarge. A villager, like you wanted," Hard-on bragged.

"Awesome," McAllister responded. "While you guys were out lollygagging we bagged at least ten of those things. They've got quite a collection of them now."

"What are they doing with them?" I asked.

"Fuck if I know," the sergeant growled back. "But one of 2nd Platoon's guys got bit bringing those fuckers in. They got him over there with Jonesy."

"Is Jonesy okay?" I solicited.

"He's still alive," McAllister responded.

"Did you get a good look at any of the other ones they brought in, Sarge?" I asked.

"Yeah, I did." he responded seriously.

"Well, are they sick, or dead? What the fuck is going on with them?" I inquired.

"We still don't know. The colonel and his men are running tests around the clock trying to figure this virus shit out. It is beyond me why he wanted all these infected brought in, but I'm just a stupid grunt. The colonel hasn't said anything to me yet, but the major's position is that these people are sick, so sick that they don't realize that they should be dead. They're too sick to die," he concluded.

"What?" I stuttered back.

"That's exactly what I said," McAllister laughed. "Don't make a lot of sense, does it?"

"Look, Sarge, I've seen dead people before, and these things we're bringing back, they're dead," I concluded.

"Dead people don't walk around," McAllister countered.

"Sarge, they're dead!" I insisted.

"This shit is something entirely new, Parsons. You're not a doctor, you're a grunt, and you'd damn well better remember it before you get yourself shot," he concluded.

"Sgt. McAllister, listen to me. The unit we came here to rescue, they're gone. You've got to know that in your heart. We are risking our lives out here for nothing!" I grumbled.

"Dying for nothing goes with the territory. Suck it up. Sometimes you're too smart for your own good," he warned me. "You guys get out to the village with the rest of 1st Platoon. We're establishing a forward perimeter. More of the locals might come in. I don't want any more fucking surprises!"

We went through decontamination again and moved out to the village. The sun was high in the afternoon sky; it beat down on us like a huge bronze hammer on a flat iron skillet. I realized that I was becoming extremely dehydrated.

We linked up with our sister squad at the chapel. They had spread out in a rough skirmish line across the village. Their squad leader, Specialist Sadler, came over to meet us.

"Man. I am glad you guys are here." He swore. "We were spread way too thin to stop anything from coming through."

"Yeah, we're thrilled to help you queers out," Hard-on replied.

Sadler ignored him. "Have you guys heard anything?" he asked. "Nobody's telling us nothing."

"No," I replied.

"But you guys shot one of them, the nurse right?" he exclaimed.

"There's something very wrong with the people who were here," I added. "We had a hell of a time killin' her. We had to shoot her to pieces."

"Damnation," Sadler cursed.

"Yeah," I replied sadly.

"Well, you guys can take the right side; we'll take the chapel and the left. At least now we can keep each other in sight. I feel way better with you guys here."

We spread out across the village. I sat in the doorway of an empty hut and sipped warm water from my canteen. At least I was in the shade. I was starting to feel sick and dizzy. Part of me panicked; I was sure I had the virus. Reality kicked in and, I realized I was just getting sunstroke; it had happened to me before. I tried to stay still and calm. Slowly, I began to feel slightly better. It had been a long day.

I tried to stay alert. I peered out between the huts before me. The superheated air shimmered before my eyes. I could swear I was seeing movement in the distance.

I blinked to clear my sight. Slowly, the hazy figures coalesced before my watering eyes into men.

The villagers were returning. They limped and hobbled forward; a lot of them.

I stumbled back to the chapel. Gunner and Hard-on were right behind me.

"They're coming back," I croaked.

"We have to hold the line," Sadler demanded. "Get back out there."

"No way, man," Hard-on responded.

The sound of gunfire came clearly to us, just from our left at the edge of the village.

"Shit," Sadler cursed. "No one is supposed to be firing! You guys need to get back out there."

The rest of Sadler's squad burst through the huts and joined us.

"What are you guys doing?" Sadler demanded. "Who was shooting out there?"

One of his men stepped up. "Some of the villagers came at us on the east side," he panted. "Something was wrong with them. I figured they had the virus, so we pulled back to avoid contact. We fired a few warning shots, but they just kept coming. What the hell are we supposed to do if we're not shooting, throw rocks at them?"

"Fuck!" Sadler growled in frustration.

"I see one!" Hard-on shouted, pointing between the huts.

"Somebody better get the Sarge or the LT on the radio and sort this shit out!" I remarked.

"Great idea," Sadler responded. "Somebody bring me the MSRT."

"Hey, you guys! They're comin' in!" somebody shouted from the left.

We moved into position at the rear of the chapel, taking cover as best we could. The main road ran directly by the chapel, and several small paths converged from the far side of the village here. Sadler's squad and ours made eight. We had two SAWs between us, and around two-hundred rounds of ammo each for the M-4s. Of course, we were under orders not to fire.

I could see several villagers slowly converging on our position. They staggered stiffly up the track. Their moans filled the air as they advanced. Every man in the platoon wanted to break and run. Only our training kept us where we were.

Sadler finally got the LT on the mobile satellite radio transmitter. They argued for a moment. "The LT wants us to hold this position. He says no one should be shooting; we are not to fire warning shots. We can only return fire if we are fired upon."

"What?" Hard-on yelled, dumbfounded.

"Tell that dumb bastard what's going on up here!" I shouted.

Sadler argued into the radio. "The LT says do not fire unless fired upon!" he repeated.

The lead villagers stumbled forward. As they closed with us, we could all plainly see that something was extremely wrong with them, that they were all fucked. The closest man to us could barely walk. One of his arms hung limp and useless at his side. His clothing was bloodstained and torn. His face was shredded so badly that I could plainly see his teeth and part of his jawbone, and he was missing an eye. The next two behind him looked even more fucked up.

"Are you guys seeing this shit?" Hard-on yelled. "They've all got the virus!"

"Shut up!" Sadler screamed. "Everyone hold your fire! The LT says do not fire!"

Everyone stood their ground as the villagers advanced; we followed our orders to the last.

The lead villager stumbled into the line. He grappled with one of Sadler's men and they went down in a twist of thrashing limbs.

"Fuck this!" Hard-on bellowed. He opened fire on the closest villager. The man crumpled under the point blank rounds, but continued to crawl forward. Hard-on stopped shooting and viciously stomped the man's head in. I could hear his victim's skull crunch under his boots.

We all opened fire on the villagers attacking us. They went down, but continued to struggle forward despite suffering wounds that would kill a normal man. All of us emptied clip after clip into the struggling corpses at our feet, until our targets were completely dismembered. Even the pieces remained animate.

The first line of attackers was down, but more were advancing through the huts towards us.

"Cease fire!" Sadler screamed.

Once we stopped shooting, I could still hear gunfire in the distance.

"Mother Mary, full of grace..." Gunner began chanting.

The LT's voice came dimly through the radio.

"Shit, we're fucked now," Sadler cursed.

He shouted into the radio, trying to explain our situation to the lieutenant over the chaos around him; everyone was talking at once.

"Everyone shut up!" I yelled.

"The LT says we can fire at our discretion, they've been attacked too!" Sadler shouted.

"That's mighty white of him, but did you tell him that shooting them doesn't seem to be doing much good?" I asked.

"Yeah, I did. The CO seems to think that they are either on drugs or really sick or some such shit. He suggested head shots," Sadler laughed.

"Typical," I responded.

"Here they come!" Hard-on warned.

The villagers staggered up the path into a hail of lead. The platoon opened up with everything we had. I saw several of them take shots center mass that would drop a linebacker. They staggered back a pace or two, and just kept coming. Quite a few of the villagers went down, their legs blown out, but they continued to crawl forward. One of them lost both arms but just kept staggering forward until Gunner turned the SAW on him. The big gun blew the man into bloody lumps. His head jumped off his shattered torso and rolled away.

I tried to concentrate on headshots. My second target took three solid shots to the head, stopping each time before coming forward again. My fourth shot decapitated the target, and he fell over into the mud. Before my unbelieving eyes, the headless corpse staggered back upright and stumbled slowly forward again, its fingers groping blindly.

A headless attacker was too much for Gunner. He stopped firing and dropped the SAW into the mud, then fell to his knees and began praying. He crossed himself repeatedly, chanting the first lines of the Lord's Prayer over and over again.

Luckily, we ran out of targets before our ammo gave out completely, but it was close. The last mobile attacker staggered towards us, dragging one shot-up, broken leg behind it. Concentrated fire from the men still fighting shredded it into bloody chunks. The other SAW raked the downed corpses until only twitching, immobile body parts remained on the blood-covered track.

"Fuck me!" Sadler gasped. "I don't believe what I just saw."

Hard-on stomped over to Gunner and shook him. "Snap out of it, asshole!" he screamed.

Gunner opened his eyes and looked around at us in shock; tears ran down his face.

"How much ammo do we have left?" I asked.

Everyone did a quick round count. We were down to about twenty-five rounds per man and a pair of two-hundred round belts for the SAWs. Two of Sadler's squad were completely out. We had shot through almost all of our ammo in a single firefight with an unarmed foe.

"I think we're in trouble," I muttered. "Sadler, you had better get the LT back on the horn and let him know how low on ammunition we are. We can't stop another attack."

Sadler contacted Command again. There was no argument this time.

"The old man wants everybody back at the HQ, pronto!"

We gladly retreated back through the village.

REPORT FROM COLONEL WARREN MEDICAL CO BRAVO

COLONEL ORTEGA'S ANALYSIS OF VIRUS CONFIRMED. AMBULATORY CADAVER SYNDROME CONFIRMED UNDER LABORATORY CONDITIONS. VIDEO TO FOLLOW.

THIS VIRUS IS EXTREMELY CONTAGIOUS.

SUGGEST IMMEDIATE QUARANTINE OF AREA AND IMPLEMENTATION OF ATTACHED SAFETY PROTOCOLS ASAP!

REPEAT ACS CONFIRMED.

MORE DETAILS AS RESEARCH PROCEEDS.

TRANSMISSION ENDS
COLONEL WARREN US ARMY MEDICAL CORP

CHAPTER 7

1:52 p.m. Zulu
Emergency Medical HQ
Village of Lat, the Congo

We returned to the far side of the village. The attack seemed to have ended; we encountered no more of the villagers as we retreated.

A sharp firefight had gone down on this side of the village too, as about a dozen of the sick villagers had emerged from the rain forest and attacked 2nd Platoon. We approached the killing ground. Hundreds of empty shell casings lay shining in the mud.

Two corpsmen from the medical unit were pushing still twitching body parts into a hastily dug fire pit nearby.

We stopped to stare. A medic came forward and inspected our suits. He asked if any of us had been bitten.

Some of the men were busy digging foxholes and stringing wire. It looked like we were staying for a while.

We could still hear the agitated moans from the samples tent. I shuddered.

I didn't see the major anywhere. It was a safe bet that he had disappeared when the shooting had started. He led from the rear.

"Let's find the Sarge," I suggested.

We found McAllister near the fire pit.

"Sarge, what are we doing here?" I asked.

"We are holding this area while Col. Warren figures out what happened," he replied.

"Maj. Dorset thinks that these people were just sick." I pointed to the smoldering bones and embers in the blackened pit. "The motherfuckers we fought were already dead, Sarge. These cock suckers are zombies!"

Sadler gave a short harsh laugh. "Zombies ain't real."

The sergeant didn't reply.

"They aren't zombies, are they, Sgt. McAllister?" Sadler asked.

"I don't know what they are," the sergeant answered. "All kinds of weird shit goes on in Africa. I'm not sure if our rules apply here."

"I'm telling you, Sarge, the people out there, the things we fought, they aren't alive anymore!" I emphasized. "But the major thinks they are. He's going to get us all killed!"

"I know the situation is fucked," the sergeant replied sadly. "But the major is in charge, what he says goes. The only good thing I can tell you is that we won't be here long. Special Forces are coming in to take over. They'll be here in two days to relieve us."

"Fuck," I muttered. "What if there are more of those things out there?"

"Then we do what we're paid to do," McAllister answered. "I don't like this any better than you do, Parsons. The only one here who can countermand the major's orders is Col. Warren, and he's still too busy looking over the shit the missing unit left behind to talk to me yet. We'll just have to wait."

"Can we at least be proactive?" I asked.

"Yea," the Sarge replied. "These fuckers ain't taken me down without a fight."

1st Platoon spent the rest of the day setting up a secure perimeter around the HQ. The major had ordered it. It was a dick move and he knew it. Physical labor in chem gear is brutal. He wanted foxholes and wire done before dark.

The work was real slow going in our biohazard gear. You could only dig for a few minutes at a time, then you had to stop and rest. As the sun moved across the sky, the heat became super intense. You could sip water through a gas mask, but you couldn't eat. It didn't take long before I felt sick again. I was starving and nauseous at the same time. My uniform was soaked with sweat, and I was constantly thirsty, no matter how much water I drank.

We had to watch out for each other constantly. The guy next to you would just pass out and fall over. As the day progressed, we lost half the platoon to heat stroke. The medical corpsmen had their hands full. Finally, I couldn't take it anymore. I staggered over into the shade of the trees and lay there panting like a dog. The next thing I knew, Sgt. McAllister was pulling off my mask. He dumped cool water over my head and handed me a canteen.

"Sip that, Parsons," he ordered.

I noticed that he wasn't wearing his chem gear.

"What gives?" I asked, pointing feebly at his regular uniform. He was down to a T-shirt and fatigue pants. "Where's your chem gear?"

"Col. Warren cleared us to operate without it," he replied. "We were about to lose everyone to heat stroke and dehydration. The colonel says he can't find any solid evidence that the virus is transmittable through the air. He thinks it's only passed through the bloodstream. We lucked out."

"Ah, shit," I muttered. "What about Jonesy?"

"It doesn't look good," the sergeant replied. "He's got a high fever. Warren told me he definitely has the virus. They're monitoring him. If the colonel can figure this shit out, he might pull through. We don't know yet."

"Damn," I answered.

"Come on," McAllister suggested, helping me to my feet. "Let's get some food in you."

As the evening wore on, the platoon slowly recovered until everyone was back in the line. We had no further visitors from the forest, everything was quiet; the calm before the storm, I figured. I wasn't looking forward to dark. Everyone was muttering quietly about what had happened. None of us had signed up to fight zombies.

We worked extra hard to improve our defensive positions. A rough box of foxholes now surrounded the tents and the motor pool, thirty yards out. Beyond that, we had strung up trip wires and flare wires, to warn us of any breaches in the line. Each side of the box had a SAW assigned to it; they were in the corners where they could provide overlapping fire to either side.

My squad drew the side of the box facing the village. I hunkered down into my foxhole and waited. I could still hear those poor bastards in the sample tent. The sound was just about enough to make you really edgy. I gritted my teeth and tried to ignore it.

I had rigged up my poncho over the hole for shade. The temperature was pretty decent without my chem gear, it felt like a balmy eighty-five or so. Everyone had been issued extra ammunition. I had a full five-hundred rounds in my hole, twenty magazines with twenty-five rounds each of 556. Thousands of rounds of extra ammo were parked just behind me near the truck.

We were down Jonesy in our squad, and 2nd Platoon had a man bitten and a man MIA. No one knew what had happened to him. I figured he was still running.

Col. Warren was going through the missing medical unit's computer files and medical charts. We weren't going anywhere until he figured something out. I knew in my gut that the entire medical unit had been infected and wandered off into the forest. It would have been way better if they had simply died, and we had found their bodies. I was pretty sure they were still out there, and that they would be back.

The LT came through on our side to check things out.

"Listen up, you guys," he began. "The major says that no one is to shoot any Army personnel who return to the lines, under any circumstances. If they appear sick, they are to be captured and brought to the HQ to be turned over to the colonel. You can fire if attacked by the locals, however, and should avoid any physical contact with them, as they may be contagious."

"Anything else we should know, LT?" Hard-on queried.

"That's it," Reid replied. "Carry on." He walked back to the HQ tent.

"Sweet Susie, what a cluster-fuck," Hard-on groaned out loud. "We can shoot the locals, but don't touch 'em. Don't shoot any of our people who have turned into zombies, and be sure to grab them!"

Hard-on had a real way with words. He was right, though. The major's order was the typical counterintuitive bullshit they were always throwing at us.

We had been assigned one of the guys from Sgt. Price's platoon; a short, red-headed Irish fuck named Fitzgerald. We called him Fitzy, of course. He was okay, but I was pretty sure he had never seen any real combat. Gordo had been put into the line on our side, too; we were pretty thin on the ground. They were on my right.

They had both seen the aftermath of the attack on 2nd Platoon, everyone knew the score.

"Hey, Parsons," Gordo yelled from his foxhole. "Which end of this thing do I point at the bad guys?"

"That's real funny," I replied. I pulled myself up out of my hole and wandered over to Gordo's position.

"Give me your rifle," I said. Gordo shrugged and handed me his M-4. Fitzy walked over to see what we were doing.

I ejected the magazine, and slowly thumbed the rounds out until it was empty.

"Only load twenty-five rounds into your mags," I instructed them. "The full thirty will cause the gun to jam sometimes. Don't ask me why."

I reloaded twenty-five rounds into the magazine, and reinserted it into the receiver. I smacked it home.

"Just look through the sight, put the red dot on your target, and then pull the trigger," I said as I turned on the gun's scope and mimicked shooting it. "Even you assholes won't be able to miss."

I handed the rifle back to Gordo. "Clean that gun like your life depends on it, because it does. If you get it muddy and don't clean it, it will jam. Do the things I just told you and you might come out okay. You too, Fitzy."

With a grunt, I got up and walked back to my position in the line. I dropped into my hole.

I wasn't real copasetic with the way things were shaping up. With Jonesy out of commission, it was really just me and Hard-on on this side of the line. After the way Gunner had froze up, I wasn't too sure about him. He was on my left in the corner hole. If we lost the SAW again during an attack, we'd all be fucked. I didn't know the guy assigned to our other corner on the right. He was with 2nd Platoon, and attached to their side of the box. Theoretically, he would be okay.

"Gunner, you doing alright over there?" I inquired.

"Yeah, man," he replied.

He had been very quiet after the attack. I figured he was ashamed of the way he had frozen up. I didn't blame him; we had all just seen some pretty fucked-up shit. You never knew how you would react to combat until you were in it. Throw in zombies and all bets were off.

I had a bad feeling we were in for a shit storm. The sun was getting really low on the horizon, and shadows were spreading through the trees.

Just before dark, Sgt. McAllister walked over and squatted down beside my hole. He had his sawed-off 12-gauge pump shotgun with him. He only carried it around when he thought the shit was about to hit the fan. Seeing that gun made me nervous.

"What's up, Sarge?" I inquired.

"How do you feel about taking a little walk with me?" he asked quietly.

"Where are we going?" I asked.

"Oh, I don't know," he replied. "Maybe through the village, maybe just a little ways into the forest on the other side. I want to see what's going on out there. I don't like waiting for the enemy to bring it to me."

"Sure," I decided. I clambered up out of my foxhole and stretched my legs. "Beats sitting around here with these numb nuts anyway."

"Hard-on, Parsons and I are going to do a quick scout," the sergeant said. "We'll come back this way, and I'll hail you before we come in. None of you assholes shoot at us. You got it?" he asked loudly.

"I got ya," Hard-on replied. "Nobody fires without my order."

I followed the Sarge away from our line and into the village. He went on point and I backed him up, slightly to his right. We advanced to the chapel. The sergeant moved ahead to look at the carnage there. He walked up to the edge of the small battleground and carefully looked around. Some of the bigger, more intact body parts were still twitching in the blood-splattered, muddy track. I could tell he was recreating the combat in his mind, looking for answers there.

I don't think he found any.

"What a cluster fuck," he muttered.

Finally, we moved through the huts around them. The sergeant slowed as we walked through the village. We encountered nothing; everything was eerily silent. McAllister held up his hand and stopped.

"Do you hear that?" he finally asked.

"I don't hear anything," I answered quietly.

"Exactly," he replied. "No animals, no insects, nothing. Come on."

He led me across the clearing surrounding the village and into the rain forest beyond. We ghosted forwards, under the dark canopy of the giant trees. The sergeant led me down a faint dirt track. I was pretty sure I could find my way back, but being in the forest made me uneasy. We glided noiselessly forward across the loam.

Suddenly, the sergeant stopped. He froze in place, and I did the same. It had become very, very dark under the trees. I couldn't see anything, but I could faintly hear movement around me. A twig snapped loudly in the darkness.

The smell washed over me like a malodorous fog of death and decay. I gagged for breath. I knew this stench; it was the smell of carrion.

I very carefully pulled my NVGs down into position over my eyes and flipped them on. Suddenly, the forest was visible, bathed in the goggle's green illuminating glow.

Walking corpses were moving slowly forward all around us. They filled the spaces between the trees for as far as I could see.

The sergeant gripped my arm in the darkness.

"Run!" he hissed.

We turned and fled for our lives through the trees, running as fast as we dared. The sound drew the zombies on behind us. Their groans suddenly filled the air, and echoed through the forest. We had found them, and they had found us.

The sergeant grabbed me just beyond the chapel. We stopped for a moment and tried to catch our breath. I removed my NVGs, and we crept forward through the huts back to our lines.

"Hard-on!" McAllister bellowed.

"Yea!" he replied faintly.

"We're comin' in!" the sergeant yelled.

I followed him at a run and dropped back into my foxhole.

The Sarge stopped beside me. "Get 'em ready, I'm going to tell the others, I'll be back!" He disappeared into the gloom.

"Talk to me!" Hard-on urged. "What's going on?"

"Get ready, everybody!" I urged, setting my spare magazines close to hand. "They're coming!"

"How many?" Gordo asked.

"All of them!" I shouted back. "Hundreds, maybe more! Get that SAW up, Gunner!"

"Fuck you, man!" he replied. "I'm ready."

I could hear activity behind us as the company braced for the attack.

Horrible groans echoed through the deserted village as the zombies advanced.

Everything was calm for half a moment, then all Hell broke loose. A flare went off, silhouetting a half-dozen zombies that were clambering over the trip wires. Our line erupted in gunfire and flame. Acrid, cordite smoke filled the air as the machine guns roared. Tracers illuminated advancing targets that jerked and danced grotesquely as they were torn to pieces by the massed fire. I fired at anything that still moved.

Gunner ran the SAW over the zombies that went down, shredding them into unrecognizable, immobile bits of tattered, bloody flesh. The big gun went through its two hundred round belt of ammo in about twenty seconds.

I slammed in a fresh magazine and threw my M-4's bolt. From my foxhole, I was at the perfect height to take out the zombie's legs.

I began to fire at my target's knees and hips. I couldn't kill them, but I could cripple them and slow them down. The downed zombies piled up before my foxhole. I systematically removed their heads as they crawled slowly forward.

For every zombie we crippled or destroyed, two more staggered forward to take its place. They swarmed forward from the village and the forest. I fired off my complete magazine and ejected the empty. I realized the SAW wasn't firing; it was too quiet on my left.

"Gunner!" I screamed as I slammed in a fresh mag. I stood up in my hole and looked down the line. The zombies had overrun us. I twisted to the left and fired off my entire magazine at the zombies streaming past me.

Sgt. McAllister pushed me back into my hole.

"Stay down!" he screamed. He tossed grenade after grenade to our left, and dropped into the hole beside me. The earth shook, and lose dirt sprayed down on top of us as the grenades went off in rapid succession.

McAllister was up and gone before I could recover. I searched frantically for a fresh magazine. I finally found one and slammed it home. I threw my bolt and stood upright in my hole.

A few random zombies were still moving nearby. I fired at each in turn until they were down and immobile. Finally, there were no more upright targets in sight.

Sgt. McAllister paced the perimeter on my left, dispatching wounded zombies with headshots, one by one with his shotgun.

Twitching, eviscerated zombie fragments littered the ground all around me. I climbed out of my hole and looked around. A shredded upper torso and partial head pulled itself slowly across the bloody ground towards me. I fired my last few rounds into its neck and shoulder joints, immobilizing it.

"Where's Gunner?" I yelled to the sergeant.

"He's gone, but the SAW is still here," he replied. McAllister lifted the battle rifle from the mud and slung it on his back.

I stepped carefully down the line to my right, avoiding the more intact pieces still moving around.

Hard-on sat in his hole. He was attempting to light a bent

cigarette, but his hands were shaking badly. Finally, he lit it and lifted it to his lips, taking a hard draw.

"I thought you quit," I remarked.

He looked up, "Yeah, well I started again today."

Just beyond us, Fitzgerald lay near his hole on his back, his eyes fixed lifelessly on the sky. His neck and arms were covered with bloody bite marks.

Gordo limped over to us, and looked around.

"Shit," he slowly drawled.

Sgt. McAllister walked over to us. "Police up all the spare ammo you can and get back on station, this shit ain't over yet. I'll have somebody bring up more ammo."

He walked away into the darkness. Random shots continued to ring out all around us.

I hunted up two magazines and climbed back down into my hole. Sure enough, more zombies continued to emerge from the village, one and two at a time. We picked them off as they came. I was down to my last few rounds when Sgt. Price moved up behind me, yelling at us to hold our fire. He had two cases of ammunition.

"I'll be back with some beers later," he joked as he ran back the way he had come.

We took turns covering each other while we reloaded all our spare magazines.

The zombies came on all night long, but we had thinned them out. They didn't break our line again.

Finally, the sun rose over the battleground, illuminating the horrid scene before our bloodshot eyes. Flopping, twitching, jiggling bits of human beings moved in heaps and piles, bits and pieces everywhere. The putrid smell was beyond description or comprehension. Blood and bile covered every inch of the mud between the village and us. I threw up into my hole.

OPS ORD 9-31

COLONEL WARREN US ARMY MEDICAL CORP BRAVO COMPANY

YOU ARE HEREBY PLACED IN COMMAND OF BRAVO COMPANY AND ORDERED TO EXTRACT ALL SPECIMENS AND DATA FOR IMMEDIATE DELIVERY TO FORT BENNING GEORGIA USA.

THIS ORDER EFFECTIVE IMMEDIATELY

ORDERS END

CHAPTER 8

06:00 a.m. Zulu
The Village of Lat
The Congo

Eventually, some of the medical guys worked their way around to our side of the square. They were wearing biological masks and coveralls. One of them started a fire, and the others labored to push the body parts into it. Greasy black smoke rose into the sky as they worked.

Sgt. McAllister relieved us to go and grab some food at the chow tent that Price's guys had set up. I was utterly exhausted. The stench of the camp was amazingly bad. I had to hold my nose while I ate, and the food tried hard to come back up.

After I had eaten, I crawled into one of the Humvees and stretched out across the jump seats. Later in the day, Hard-on came and found me.

"Come on, asshole," he said. "The colonel's going to brief everybody. He says it's important."

"Alright," I groaned. I climbed out of the vehicle and groggily followed him over to the command tent. Most of the company was already there. Everyone tried to ignore the sounds and the stench emanating from the sample tent.

The old man and Lt. Beckham were seated near the tent; everyone else was just standing around, waiting for the colonel.

Finally, the colonel stepped through the tent flap. The major and the LT stood up.

"At ease," the colonel stuttered, waving them back to their seats. He looked pretty rough. I realized he probably hadn't slept since we had arrived.

"I called you men together to share what I've learned with you," he began. "I understand we've already suffered some casualties, and I want you to know the stakes, what we are fighting for, and what we are up against."

He paused for a moment. "I've gone through all the records the medical unit's commanding officer left behind. His name was Colonel Ortega. The colonel had identified the virus they were sent here to contain, and was working on an anti-virus, or serum. Unfortunately, he failed to complete it before his own death. All the people originally from this village contracted the virus and died. I believe that they are the people who have returned and attempted to attack us. I am now convinced that these same locals attacked Ortega and his staff, and killed them all."

The colonel paused again to cough, then he continued. "As difficult as it has been for me to accept, apparently this virus causes some sort of physical reanimation of dead tissue in its victims, in order to spread and propagate itself. I would have considered this as medically impossible, if I hadn't verified it myself under laboratory conditions and in the field, as you men have. Colonel Ortega had termed this condition Ambulatory Cadaver Syndrome. That name is as good as any."

I smiled smugly. I was right. My smile faded as I realized that might not be such a good thing.

One of the transport guys spoke up, "No offense, sir, but are you telling us that the people attacking us are really dead, that they are zombies?"

The colonel sighed loudly. "I don't know that I would technically call them zombies, but yes, they are dead, reanimated cadavers. These creatures retain no real brain activity; they are mindless. From a security perspective, they will be no real threat to a fully armed combat company. A headshot should disable their remaining senses. When you combat these creatures, you must simply remember to fire disabling shots. Target the joints; shoulders, knees, hips, and neck, or remove the limbs and head entirely. The virus is driving these dead bodies to attack the living in order to spread itself into new host material. A bite, a scratch, any fluid transfer will spread the virus to a new host. You must avoid any unprotected physical contact with these creatures. Their remains are an extreme biohazard. They must be burned immediately."

"What about the men who were bitten, Colonel?" I asked.

"As of now, all of our personnel who were bitten have been placed in quarantine, under restraint. I am working on the problem, but the virus is fatal once contracted. The incubation time is extremely fast if the virus enters the bloodstream through an open wound. Anyone bitten must be admitted to my care immediately, they will become a danger to everyone around them."

I didn't need to ask about Jonesy; I knew now that he was dead.

"Our mission to rescue the medical corps is no longer viable. I have five members of the original unit we were sent here to secure, two that were captured during the attack last night. These were American servicemen, not locals, who were among the reanimated dead. I have examined them, and they are dead. They have been dead for days. It is my opinion that the medical unit was killed to a man. Those who were not completely devoured reanimated and wandered away, until we arrived here."

I was happy to hear this. It meant that our mission was over and we could get out of this hellhole. I thought that the colonel would announce that next.

"These creatures will continue to attack us as long as we remain here. Our own casualties will become a threat if their bodies are not destroyed. But we must remain here. I need more time, time to complete Ortega's work. This virus is not just a danger to us; it is a threat to Africa and really to the whole world. I don't know how far the virus has spread, but our best hope is to complete Ortega's work," he concluded wearily.

The major stepped up to speak. "We will be relieved by Special Forces within forty-eight hours. Our mission has changed; it has not ended. You men will hold our perimeter and protect the medical unit so that the colonel can continue his work. Dismissed!"

Some asshole called us all to attention. The officers ducked back into the tent. Everyone began to wander away, most complaining bitterly.

Even I had to admit; asking us to hang around to handle a virus and zombies was pretty far off our normal radar. I wasn't even sure if we were drawing hazardous duty pay.

I found a semi-private place to drop a deuce, then I walked back by the mess tent and grabbed a couple of MRE packets and some coffee. I would have them away from the stench of the camp.

I wandered back over to my foxhole. It looked like I would be calling it home for at least a couple more days. I said a quick prayer that it wouldn't rain.

Sgt. McAllister was sitting with Hard-on. They were smoking and drinking beers. It looked like Price had been by. I joined them, squatting on the muddy ground nearby. I spread out a dirty uniform shirt and broke down my M-4, laying the parts on it. I cleaned and oiled the receiver and the bolt while we talked.

"Jonesy is dead, isn't he, Sarge?" I asked, not looking up.

"Yeah," McAllister replied sadly. "He died during the night."

"Did he come back?" I asked hesitantly.

"Don't know," the sergeant replied. "They're not letting anybody back there, where they keep the casualties. I know he was a friend of yours. Try not to think about it. Just remember him the way he was."

I didn't say anything for a minute. I cleaned my gun's barrel and began to reassemble it. "What about Gunner? Did you find him?"

"Parts of him I think," McAllister replied grimly. "It looked like they pulled him outta his hole and tore him to pieces. At least we don't have to worry about him coming back."

"He was a mean, little fat bastard," Hard-on intoned. He lifted his beer. "Here's to Gunner."

He and the sergeant drank a toast.

I wouldn't miss Gunner, but I wished he hadn't gotten himself killed. Every man that died in your squad brought you that much closer to your own death.

They tossed me a beer. I opened it and drank to Gunner.

"And to Jonesy!" I added.

We all toasted him too.

"They burned Fitzy. At least they didn't just toss him in with the zombies," Hard-on added.

"Don't make no difference," McAllister opined. "Once you're dead, you're gone." He tapped his thick shoulder. "This is just a shell of flesh and bone. Your soul goes on."

"You believe in that shit, Sarge, Heaven and Hell?" Hard-on laughed.

"I'd believe in Hell if I was you, Hard-on," the sergeant laughed back. "You'll be there soon enough. If they cremate your nasty ass, it'll just give you a head start."

"The only motherfucker in this outfit who had any religion was Gunner. Fat lot of good it did him," Hard-on observed.

"We'll all find out what's waitin' on the other side if we don't get out of this village pretty soon," I grunted.

"Always the optimist," McAllister laughed.

"I'm serious, Sarge," I replied. "Isn't there anything you can do?"

"I'm not in charge here, Parsons, you know that," he answered.

"This is just nuts," I complained. "I think the colonel has lost his mind."

"What are you talking about?" Hard-on asked.

"Anything he's doing here, he could do back in the real world," I pointed out. "He's working out of a tent, with field equipment. He needs to be in a real lab. This is all bullshit!"

"There you go again," McAllister warned. "Don't talk like that where anyone else can hear you. The major is still gunning for you."

"You know I'm right," I continued. "And I'll tell you something else. I think those fuckers he's keeping in his 'sample tent' are attracting the others to us."

The low moans from the sample tent echoed eerily across the camp to us.

"That noise is driving me crazy," I groaned.

"Suck it up, and keep your pie hole shut," the sergeant barked.

McAllister stood up and stretched. "I'll be back," he grunted.

"Where ya going, Sarge?" Hard-on asked.

"I'm going to talk to the old man. We need to be doin' something besides just waiting around."

We hung out in our foxholes. There wasn't much else to do. Grey clouds began to move across the afternoon sky, threatening rain. I began to grow drowsy. It was still very warm, and I had a hard time staying awake. I was just about to nod off when Sgt. McAllister and Gordo walked over to our line. The Sarge had his shotgun with him, and Gordo was carrying an M-4. They approached my hole. I groaned and climbed out to meet them.

The sergeant had a folded topo map in his hand. He showed it to me.

"We are here. There is another village about three miles from here, closer to the Congo River." He pointed to them with his finger.

"I want to do a quick scout and see if they've been hit with the virus. We need to get a handle on what's going on around us," he informed me.

I groaned.

"I'm taking you and Gordo," he laughed.

"Why me?" I inquired.

"I don't want you to stir up any more shit while I'm gone," he answered. "At least this way, I can keep an eye on you."

"Fuck," I replied.

"You'd better bring your poncho," the sergeant suggested, pointing to the thickening cloud cover. "I think it's going to rain."

We left the village and trudged into the rain forest. The sergeant knew where he was going. He led us to the trail on which we had encountered the first zombie. We took the split to the left and followed it deeper into the trees. The sergeant took point, with Gordo in the middle and me at the rear.

"Stay sharp," the Sarge warned.

He moved forward on the faint trail at a quick walk, scanning the foliage around us. The forest was alive with all of its normal sounds. Monkeys and birds chirped and screeched in the treetops, insects buzzed and droned.

We didn't see any sign of zombies once we moved away from the village.

McAllister led us onward. He stopped occasionally to listen, or peer into the brush. I didn't notice anything unusual. The massive trees filled the world on both sides of the dim trail. Their trunks formed dim corridors that led away into the green gloom. They didn't look inviting to me. I wished for a breath of fresh air. The interlocking canopy of branches and leaves overhead blocked out the sky and sealed out the wind. The air was heavy, moist, and laden with the smell of the trees. I didn't like it.

We walked onward through the forest. The path labored up a series of small hills, and then wound down into a valley. The sergeant checked his map.

"The village is at the bottom, be ready," he warned.

We moved slowly forward, scanning the trees and foliage around us. Nothing seemed amiss, nothing happened.

The forest trail emerged from the trees and we were left standing on a small bald knob. The stony path led down the barren hillside, through a tiny, thatch hut village, and ended at the Congo River.

Sgt. McAllister stopped to look around. The place looked a lot like the village we had left behind. There were no people, no activity, nothing at all, just empty huts.

"Let's check it out," he suggested.

We entered the village and carefully searched for any sign of its inhabitants. The small thatch and clapboard huts were empty. This village didn't have a church or a clinic to search. We could pretty well guess what had happened. All we found were bloodstains and footprints in the mud.

We approached the river. A few log canoes were drawn up on the muddy riverbank. We stopped at the riverside and stared at the swirling, muddy waters.

Suddenly, Gordo jerked his head around. He lifted his gun and looked wildly around.

"What is it?" McAllister hissed.

I couldn't see or hear anything.

"There," Gordo whispered. He pointed to the forest beyond the canoes. "Listen."

I listened carefully. I could faintly hear a low moaning.

Sgt. McAllister moved to the left. He waved us back behind him and glided noiselessly forward through the trees. I moved up to support him, behind and to his right. I lifted my gun to my shoulder, and slowly advanced.

The sergeant stopped and lowered his shotgun. "Gordo, get up here."

We advanced until we were beside the sergeant. A withered old man sat in the mud before us, cradling a muddy straw doll. He rocked back and forth with his eyes closed, moaning softly.

"Try to talk to him, Gordo," the sergeant whispered.

Gordo crept forward. He slowly reached out to gently touch the old man's arm.

The man's eye's fluttered open. He looked around, but he didn't seem to register anything.

Gordo spoke softly to him in Congolese. The old man muttered and moaned.

"Ask him what happened here," McAllister suggested.

Gordo translated. He repeated his question again.

The old man finally replied.

"He says the old ones came back. The dead," Gordo whispered.

"What does he mean?" McAllister asked.

Gordo questioned the old man. He replied in mutters, sobbing softly.

"I don't know, Sergeant," Gordo said, shaking his head. "He is saying something about the dead coming from the trees. It doesn't make any sense. I think he has lost his mind."

"Ask him where the people are, the villagers who lived here," McAllister urged.

Gordo translated the question.

The old man lifted his arm. He pointed shakily into the forest. He mumbled a single word.

Gordo stood up. "He said gone."

We didn't find any other survivors. Gordo suggested that we bring the old man with us, but McAllister told him no. The sergeant wanted to get back to our camp as fast as we could, the elderly man would only slow us down.

We left the village behind us and raced back along the trail. Lightning flashed in the distance, and it grew noticeably darker as we moved into the trees. We walked as fast as we could, practically at a jog. We were about half way back when the wind picked up and the rain hit. Fat, warm drops spattered down past the canopy and ran in rivulets from the leaves overhead. We paused long enough to put on our ponchos.

"Shit, this is really going to slow us down," the sergeant complained.

We forged ahead through the storm. As he had predicted, the trail quickly turned into a muddy quagmire of sucking black mud. Our pace slowed as we progressed.

Lightning flashed through the treetops, and thunder rolled back to us from the west. The sergeant stopped and held us back. He knelt in the trail, and reached back to pull us down. The rain fell in buckets and I couldn't see shit.

"What is it, Sarge?" I whispered.

"Ten o'clock, ahead of us, and two," he hissed back at me.

I peered ahead through the deluge. Lightning flashed, illuminating the forest. For a split second, I could see.

Zombies were moving slowly ahead of us through the trees. Dozens of them were just forward of our position to either side of the trail, moving away from us, back towards our camp.

"What's the plan?" Gordo inquired in a hushed voice.

"They're going to hit the camp again," the sergeant replied. "We need to get back there ahead of them to warn the others. When I give the word, run. Stay on the trail, I'll fall back a little to make sure you guys get through. Don't look back. That's an order."

I tensed.

"Go!" McAllister urged.

Gordo and I sprinted down the muddy trail. I slipped in the muck and almost went down. I knew if I did, I was dead. I recovered and scrambled on. I couldn't see them, but I could feel the zombies on either side reaching out through the pouring rain to grab me. Gordo was faster than me, and he pulled ahead on down the trail. We slipped through them in the deluge, and ran for our lives.

I ran until I was winded and had to stop. Gordo had disappeared into the forest ahead of me. I heard McAllister's shotgun go off through the trees behind me, again and again. I had just decided to go back and look for him when the sergeant burst through the falling rain and almost ran me down.

"What are you doing, Parsons?" he shouted. "Run!"

We ran through the driving rain and the mud until we reached the village. We trudged through to the other side and reentered our perimeter lines. Gordo was already there in his foxhole. Hard-on waved to me.

"I told them!" Gordo shouted.

"Great!" McAllister shouted back. He ran on into the camp. I dropped into my foxhole. It had already partially filled with muddy warm water, that sloshed into my already wet boots.

"This sucks!" I screamed to the uncaring skies. It began to rain harder.

Sgt. McAllister sloshed back to our side of the square. His arms were full of small green rectangular boxes. I recognized them immediately. He had brought back about a dozen Claymore mines. He wasn't fucking around anymore.

He sloshed past me towards the village. "Cover me!" he shouted back.

I could barely see him through the downpour. Lightning flashed and the thunder rolled. The storm broke upon us in all its tropical fury. The wind whipped up, scattering debris and leaves, and driving the rain into my eyes.

I stood in my foxhole and brought my rifle up to my shoulder. I was careful to keep my finger off the trigger. I scanned the huts beyond the sergeant for any sign of movement.

McAllister struggled through the mud, hastily setting each mine into the muck, and stringing the detonator line out to the mine beside it. He daisy chained the mines together in pairs, moving left to right, setting a twosome and then moving closer to our line, and setting another pair.

The sergeant armed the last pair directly before us, only twenty feet away, and ran back.

He knelt beside me and yelled in my ear, "I'm going to be on the left corner with the SAW. Watch the right side! If you're overrun, fall back to the Humvees if you're able. Luck!"

He disappeared into the rain.

OPS ORD 9-45

SPECIAL FORCES UNIT TO RELIEVE BRAVO COMPANY ENROUTE

ARMY OFFICER CAPTAIN TUCKER, SAMUEL, J. TO ASSUME COMMAND
IMMEDIATE

SECURE ALL SAMPLES AND DATA, STAND BY FOR EVACUATION

ORDERS END

CHAPTER 9

05:58 p.m. Zulu
Medical Unit HQ
The Congo

I stood in the pouring rain and waited. I knew the zombies were out there, just beyond the first huts, moving towards us through the village. Time slowed to a crawl and seemed to stop. The stress of combat did weird things to your perceptions.

My straining eyes began to imagine zombies everywhere. My finger tightened on the trigger, but I didn't have a clear target. No one else was firing. The lightning illuminated the killing zone between the huts and our line; it was still clear.

"Come on, you fuckers," I growled. I rubbed my eyes and covered them with my hand, attempting vainly to keep the rain out of my sight.

A lightning bolt hit the trees just outside the village. The brilliant white light blinded me for a second. The thunder broke almost simultaneously as the first zombie hit the lead Claymore's trip wire. A bright red flash overlaid the white afterimages flickering in my eyes, and a deafening roar filled my ears. I dimly heard the SAW shooting to my left.

I followed the tracers out to the zombies who were streaming out of the village and onto the killing ground. Many of them were down, their legs blown off or shattered by the Claymores. They struggled to stand or pull themselves forward. I fired off a full magazine at anything that still moved.

Zombie after zombie staggered forward from between the bullet-riddled huts. I ejected my empty and slammed in a fresh magazine. The lead zombie on my right hit another Claymore wire. The mines went off in a simultaneous wave of destruction, shattering everything before them with seven-hundred screaming steel balls. The zombies were flung back in a crimson flash of mutilation. The closest were eviscerated and shredded beyond the endurance of the human body. They didn't rise again. Those farthest away were only crippled or knocked down. They struggled towards us, pulling themselves along with their broken limbs on ripped open bellies. The Claymores went off to my left with a flash and a roar.

Someone threw a flare onto the battlefield. It illuminated a scene straight from the deepest pits of Hell in a flickering white light. Everywhere I looked partial cadavers and crippled, bullet-riddled zombies struggled to pull themselves forward across a wriggling, squirming, moving carpet of dismembered bloody human body parts.

I screamed in horror and defiance. I began to systematically fire into the heads of the closest zombies, splattering the mud with chunks of slimy grey brain matter.

Still, the fuckers came on. They stumbled, they slithered, they stumped, and they crawled.

A partial cadaver wiggled into the wire strung between the last two Claymores. The shockwave tossed me back into my hole. Everything directly before me was lifted and flung backwards, utterly destroyed. The steel ball bearings threw up small splash holes in the blood-soaked ground. I slid down into my foxhole, momentarily stunned.

The rain poured down on me and brought me awake. Someone grabbed me by my webbing's shoulder strap and tried to haul me up out of my hole. I looked up and pissed myself. A one-armed, disemboweled zombie was trying to pull me up towards his snapping, broken teeth. I wedged my M-4 between us and pulled the trigger. The zombie disintegrated into rotting, gory chunks. Its thrashing legs slid into the hole with me.

I fled the foxhole, pulling myself out and back across the slimy mud. The thing's hand still clung spider-like to my harness until I pulled it loose and flung it away. I lay trembling in the mud.

The rain washed over me. I knew I should get up, that I should reload my gun and get back into the fight. Somehow, I didn't care anymore.

Dimly over the ringing in my ears, I heard someone shouting my name. I looked around in confusion.

Hard-on was standing beside me. He blasted a legless crawling cadaver that was almost on top of me, and kicked it away back into the muck.

"Get up!" he screamed at me.

He pulled me to my feet, and led me back away from the line. We retreated towards the tents. Someone helped me sit down in the mud, and then everything went black.

When I came to, it had stopped raining and the sun was up. It felt like early morning. I sat upright and put a hand to the back of my head. A bandage was wound around my dome. I could feel a goose egg under the wrappings. I was on an Army cot inside a tent. One of the flaps was tied back. The smell of rotting meat hit me; I gagged and panicked. For a split-second, I thought I was in the sample tent. I looked around wildly.

No one else was with me. I slowly sat upright and swung my legs over the side, gingerly got up, and stumbled outside. The bright sunlight hurt my eyes.

"Look who's alive," Sgt. McAllister joked. He was standing near the Humvees with Sgt. Price and Hard-on. I slowly limped over to join them.

"What happened?" I asked.

"I've been getting that a lot this morning," the sergeant replied. "Hard-on brought you back off the line. It was a mess out there, but the Claymores broke up most of the concentrated attack. The fuckers are still coming in though."

A rifle went off nearby.

"See," the sergeant pointed out.

"Please tell me we are pulling out now," I pleaded.

"The officers are discussing that as we speak," McAllister replied. "I suggested it, but it hasn't been decided yet. At this point, I think even the old man is ready to go."

"Did we lose anybody?" I asked.

"Oh yea," the sergeant rejoined grimly. "They got Lt. Reid. Hell, we suffered fifty percent casualties between 1st and 2nd platoons.

You and Hard-on are it for your squad; even some of the mechanics and medics who weren't in the lines bought it. Things got real bad last night. Some of those fuckers broke through the perimeter and wandered around in here for a while before I could clear 'em out. I think the major is pretty shook up."

"Good," I replied.

"Well, we will see," McAllister countered. "The colonel has the final word, and I didn't see him fighting any zombies." He walked away.

"Thanks, Hard-on," I mumbled.

"For what? Last night? Forget it, man. You would have done the same for me," he said. "Come on, you've got to see this shit."

Hard-on led me back through camp to our foxholes. The ground beyond was blasted and burned. Everywhere I looked jumbles of fire-blackened human bones protruded from the churned-up, muddy ground. I wrinkled my nose. It smelled like a cannibal barbeque gone horribly wrong; a mixture of gasoline, burnt-rotten meat, and bloody shit.

"Wow," I finally uttered. "Did we do all that?"

"Some of it," Hard-on replied. "There were so many shot-up zombie pieces out there this morning that they finally just dumped gas on everything and let it burn. You should have seen 'em wiggle. Man, did it stink."

"You know, I think Gunner may have been right," I muttered.

"What do you mean?" Hard-on asked.

"I think this place is cursed," I replied.

I limped around the perimeter of the camp, looking for some place to escape the smell. It was no use; the foul, rotten stench permeated everything, and hung in the air. I could taste it.

I passed a sniper positioned on each side of the square, sited there to shoot the occasional zombie that still wandered out of the rain forest. The area beyond the perimeter on each side of the camp was a disaster zone. The muddy earth was burned and blasted. Everywhere I looked, broken human bones protruded from the scorched earth. I wondered what the UN would think of this mess.

Even with my hands over my ears, I could still faintly hear the moans of the specimens the colonel was keeping in the sample tent to experiment on. I was absolutely convinced that the noise was attracting more zombies from the forest all around us. I was also pretty sure the colonel had lost his grip on reality. He didn't seem to have a fucking clue about what was going on out here.

The whole situation was absolutely insane.

Finally, I wandered over to the Humvees and collapsed against one of their oversized tires. I considered my options. They were slim. I even thought about desertion. I could steal a Humvee and make a run for it. At this point, I seriously doubted that anyone would even shoot at me, or bother to come after me. The only problem was that I didn't really have any place to go. I was in the middle of the DRC. The only thing for miles in every direction was more rainforest, more zombies, and the rebels.

I was fucked.

My only chance to escape was to convince Sgt. McAllister that we should leave. The major hated my guts; he would feed me to the zombies if he got the chance. Talking to him was out. I couldn't talk to the colonel and I didn't think it would do any good, anyway. He seemed determined to stay until we were all dead. Lt. Reid was gone and Lt. Beckham wouldn't support me against the major.

McAllister had access to all of the officers, and they would listen to him carefully. He was the senior NCO, and the officers respected his experience and opinion. The only problem was that he played too damn straight and by the rules. He was old school Army. He would obey an order if it killed him, literally.

I respected him for that; the only problem was it was going to get me killed too, and that wasn't going to work out for me.

Finally, I got my head together and walked back into the camp. I noticed there weren't as many personnel moving around as there had been before; all the more reason to blow this place.

I found Hard-on and Sadler at the mess tent. I took them aside and talked to them about my plan.

They were both for leaving, but wanted me to do the talking, and take the heat, as usual.

I finally got them to agree to back me up with McAllister.

We found the sergeant at the supply tent. He and Sgt. Price were sitting at an improvised table, drinking beers and smoking. They had set up an empty crate for a table, and were sitting on stacked ammunition boxes. They both looked up as we entered the tent.

"Is this a private party or can anyone come in?" I asked.

"Enter," McAllister grunted.

We squeezed inside. Sgt. Price handed us each a warm beer. He passed Hard-on a cigarette.

"Is this one mishanga, or on the house?" Hard-on asked.

"These are on me," Price answered.

Sgt. McAllister lit a cigar, pulled on it and exhaled. The smoke helped to dampen the stench of the camp. He looked us over.

"We want to talk to you, Sarge," I started.

"Ah, the inevitable mutiny," McAllister laughed. "Let me guess, you pussies have had enough and you want to go home."

Hard-on and Sadler looked down at the ground, but I looked him straight in the eye.

"None of us signed on for this shit," I shot back. "Motherfucking zombies, a virus. Come on, Sarge."

"Feel free to speak your mind, Parsons," the sergeant encouraged me. "Get it all out of your system."

"I think this whole mission has passed beyond sanity and straight to bullshit," I said bluntly. "We cannot hold this camp against another attack! Half the company is dead! Look around, Sarge. Our mission here is over. It was over before we got here. We are defending an untenable position so that the colonel can play doctor with a bunch of walking corpses! The major doesn't have the balls to do anything about it. If we don't leave, we are all gonna die here," I concluded.

"I think you're right," McAllister replied. To my surprise, he didn't get angry or rebuke me. He just sat there and puffed on his cigar.

"So, we're leaving?" I asked.

"Didn't say that," he pointed out. "I agree with most everything you said, but we're still going to follow orders. We are going to defend this camp until we are relieved, or we die. That is what you swore to do when you enlisted."

"Sarge..." I began.

McAllister interrupted me, "Parsons, you're smart enough to figure out why we are going to stay here. It doesn't have anything to do with how fucked up the orders are, or what makes sense, or even how deep in the shit we all are. It's about honor, and duty. It is to make sure your friend Jonesy, the LT, and the others didn't die for nothing. I'm sure you'll do the right thing. Just do me a favor, and stop bitching about it. Bitch, bitch, bitch, it's all you fuckers do. I'm not your fucking Mother!"

That shut me up for a minute.

"You're not the first smart-assed punk to ever question orders, Parsons," the sergeant laughed. "And you don't know everything. I got more tricks up my sleeve than a cat's got whiskers. You might live through this mess, yet. You boys help me and Sgt. Price drink some beer and whiskey. We'll put our heads together and see if we can figure this shit out."

I knew if I couldn't convince the Sarge to pull out, then I was stuck. I'd just have to make the best of it.

We sat in the tent and drank and smoked. No one bothered us for a while. We tried to talk about other shit to take our minds off our problems, but eventually, we all stopped trying.

"Has anybody even talked to the brass," I asked. "Does anyone outside Africa even know what's going down here?"

"Sure," McAllister answered. "The colonel and the major have both talked to the Pentagon. I guarantee you they are very interested in what's happening here. Don't change a damn thing. They can't send us anything fast enough to make any difference."

"What about air support?" I asked hopefully.

"Nope," the sergeant replied. "Takes too long to get here, and there ain't no local assets to call on. The flyboys couldn't hit anything but the village anyway for all the trees. I wouldn't trust the major or Beckham to call in an air strike regardless. We'd all be killed by friendly fire. Do not bring that shit up around them, I don't want them getting any bright ideas."

"How are we holding up for ammo?" I asked.

"Sgt. Price and I were just discussing that when you pecker heads showed up," McAllister replied. "We're getting kinda' low on everything."

"It ain't pretty," Price nodded.

"How bad is it?" I inquired.

"Well, we are down to one functional Platoon, and since I don't have to supply as many troops, we've got about five or six-hundred rounds of 556 NATO left per trooper. About enough for one good firefight," Sgt. Price responded. "If you fuckers could shoot straight and didn't waste so much ammo, we wouldn't be in this fix. We done burned through enough ammo to kill half a fucking division!"

"Those bastards don't lay down and die when you shoot 'em, do they now boys?" McAllister laughed.

"Fuck, no," Hard-on agreed.

"What about ammo for the SAWs?" I asked.

"That's a real tragedy," Price sighed. "We only have six cases of ammo left. Those guns could go through that real quick."

"The SAWs are the most effective weapon we have left," McAllister stated. "We'll have to use them wisely."

"I've got a half a case of nine-millimeter for the Berettas and a few boxes of shotgun shells," Price added.

"Can't we run back to the planes and pick up some more?" Hard-on inquired.

"I can't raise anyone at the insertion point on the radio," Sgt. McAllister answered slowly. "And we can't send a single vehicle, it's too dangerous. We all leave or we all stay."

We were all quiet for a moment. "What about Claymores?" I finally asked.

"We've got four left," he answered sadly.

"How we fixed for grenades?" Sadler queried.

"One case left of fragmentation, that's a dozen, and there are two white phosphorus left," Price responded. "We've got more bottles of whiskey than grenades."

"Normally, that would be a good thing," McAllister concluded. He paused to think for a moment. "Do we have any C-4 with us?"

"Nope," Price answered. "I don't like to haul that shit around unless I have to."

"How much gasoline do we have left?" the sergeant asked.

"Not much of that. I've usually got four Jerry cans full, but we've used most of it up burning the dead. Now, we've got plenty of diesel. I've got a full fifty-gallon drum in the truck and there is another ten to fifteen gallons in each of our vehicles. Of course, we need that to drive out of here back to the planes. There is a lot of diesel still in the Humvees the medical unit drove in here. Their tanks hold twenty-five gallons, full. I bet I could siphon out another forty gallons or so from them. Why do you ask?" Price wanted to know.

"There is a lot of wicked shit you can do with flammable liquids," McAllister responded. "Especially when the guys you're fighting ain't none too smart."

"Does diesel burn?" Hard-on asked.

"Fuck yeah it burns!" Price responded. "It just has a lower flash point than gasoline. It's safer, but it will still burn like hell if you get it started."

"What do you have in mind, Sarge?" I asked eagerly.

"You'll see," he responded with a wicked grin.

As our little party broke up, I took the sergeant aside. "Can I talk to you for a second?" I asked.

"Sure," he grunted back. The beers had mellowed us both a little.

"You want to hear my theory on why we are being attacked?" I suggested.

"I guess," McAllister replied. "I'll hear it sooner or later anyway."

I laughed and then grew quickly serious. "I think all the noise from the colonel's sample tent is drawing in more zombies. They seem to start moaning more when they get excited, and then that attracts even more of them. That's all that those poor bastards in that tent do. Plus all the gunfire and racket we are making killin' the ones that do show up. Hell, out here I bet a gunshot carries for miles. There's nothing else making any noise except for the birds and shit. The colonel said the virus drives them to attack living things; I bet it's like we're ringing the dinner bell for those fuckers. I think we are just sitting here like a big juicy buffet."

McAllister grunted, "I hadn't thought about that. I was too busy trying to figure out a way to beat 'em. Not bad, Parsons."

"It's just a theory," I responded.

"I'll see what I can do about the sample tent anyway," the sergeant stated.

A series of gunshots rang out from the edge of camp.

"I think it's too late to worry about the other," McAllister added.

I paused for a few seconds then spoke again, "Sarge, as lethal as this shit is, we could be the only living humans for miles. If they can sense us somehow, they're just gonna' keep on coming. We haven't actually killed that many yet, maybe just a couple three hundred."

"What's your point, Parsons?' he asked.

"I don't know what this part of the world's population is like, but there could be a lot more of them out there, maybe so many that we won't be able to stop them next time. They seem to be comin' in waves. I think they'll hit us again tonight, real hard," I concluded.

"Yeah," McAllister slowly spoke. "I'm afraid you're right about that, too. Well, we will do what damage we can with what we have to hand. Come on, we need to get to work, especially if your theory is correct!"

McAllister rounded up everyone who wasn't nailed down to make up a work detail. We walked back out to the perimeter line facing the village. The sergeant studied the ground for a moment. He walked past our foxholes a few paces and turned to face us.

"You guys are gonna' love this one," he explained. "I need a slit trench about three feet deep all the way around our perimeter line."

No one responded for a few seconds, then Hard-on realized what that meant.

"Damn it, Sarge, we done fought and sweated and dug in and searched all to fuck and back. It's too damn hot to dig!" he demanded. He looked close to tears.

McAllister responded calmly, "I know you guys are tired. Just do the best you can. We need to get as much done as humanly possible, and quickly. More of those fucks are comin' in, and we are seriously low on ammo. I'm improvising a defensive system to make up for it. This trench will keep you alive. I've got to go talk to the CO, and get a few things taken care of. I'll be back to help you as quick as I can!"

The sergeant walked back into the camp and disappeared.

Nobody wanted to dig, but we went to it. Everybody bitched and moaned. We quickly stripped down to our boots and pants. We were filthy, tired, and sore, but we dug in. The ground was just a sodden muddy mess that clung to your shovel's blade. The sun beat down on our backs; the sweat ran in buckets. We all knew that we would never finish the trench before dark, it was too damn much, but we were determined to try.

Hard-on paused for a second to chug a warm bottled water. He looked over at me and spat into the mud. "I'd give my left nut for a bulldozer about now," he grunted.

I dug another three spades-full before his words sank in. "Wait a minute," I laughed.

I looked down the shallow muddy trench. Sgt. Price was just down the line from us, digging just like everyone else. I dropped my spade and walked over to him.

"Sgt. Price, I just got an idea," I stated.

He looked up, "It had better be good."

"You'll dig it," I replied. "I know where a backhoe is."

Hard-on and I grabbed our rifles and led Sgt. Price out into the forest to the clearing where we had found the truck and the backhoe. We moved carefully; an occasional zombie was still wandering into camp, but we encountered nothing.

Price approached the derelict tractor and shook his head sadly.

"I can't do nothing with this thing, boys. It's plumb shot to shit," he intoned. "Hell, even if it ran, it wouldn't be able to move." He pointed to the backhoe's oversized tires. They had rotted and sunk into the African mud.

"Couldn't it run on the rims?" I asked hopefully.

"In this mud? Nope," he replied.

We stood looking forlornly at the beat-up backhoe.

"Wait, we really don't need to drive it around, right?" I asked.

"What do you mean?" Sgt. Price asked. "Of course you need to drive it."

"No," I retorted. "We could winch it out with the truck, and pull it back to camp. If you can get the engine to run, we could use the claw to dig the trenches. We could move it with the winch, or I've seen operators pull a backhoe along with just the arm!" I stated.

"Damn me, you're right," Price cursed. "The arm works off the PTO and hydraulics."

He looked at the backhoe's claw. "These hydraulic hoses are rotted, but I might be able to cobble something together. It's worth a shot!"

I fist bumped Hard-on. "Let's get the fucking truck."

We brought the cargo truck from the village down the path to the clearing. It barely fit between the new growth trees. We finally got it into position and hooked up our heaviest tow chain to the eight-ton winch.

"Come on, baby!" Sgt. Price chanted, over and over. He threw the winch's handle forward. We all stood clear in case the cable snapped. The winch wined and smoked, and the truck crabbed forward until it jammed against a tree trunk. Finally, with a nasty slurping sound, the backhoe pulled free and began to limp slowly back towards the truck.

Sgt. McAllister and half the camp came out to watch us as we emerged from the trees. The sergeant shook his head in wonder and ordered everybody back to work.

We reset the winch and the truck a dozen times before we had the backhoe clear and into position. Sgt. Price and two of his mechanics went to work on the tractor's engine and arm. Hard-on and I went back into the trench, and started digging again.

I was almost too numb to notice that all I could hear was the snick of the shovels, and the birds and animal noises from the forest. Suddenly, it hit me that I could hear the buzz of the ever-present flies. The moaning noise from the sample tent had ceased.

"Hey, Hard-on." I grinned. "Listen."

"Yeah, I know," he replied.

Two hours of hard digging later, I heard the high-pitched whine of a starter. We all stopped digging. I fell to my knees in the clinging mud and said a prayer for that starter to work. It sounded again, turning over and over, then stopped.

I heard Sgt. Price cursing like a San Francisco pimp, and then the starter reengaged. The backhoe's engine roared to life with a backfire and a belch of black smoke. It was the sweetest sound I had ever heard. All down the line, everyone cheered and threw down their shovels.

Two hours later, the slit trench was done.

BRAVO COMPANY SUPPLY NCO SGT PRICE

REQUEST IMMEDIATE AIR DROP OF AMMUNITION AND HEAVY MUNITIONS OUR LOCATION. SITUATION CRITICAL.

TRANSMISSION ENDS

SERGEANT PRICE US ARMY

CHAPTER 10

06:56 p.m. Zulu
Village of Lat
The Congo

Hard-on and I wrestled the fifty-gallon drum of diesel fuel into position at the lip of the trench. Its contents shifted and sloshed as we slowly lowered it down until it was horizontal, with one end overhanging the channel. We stood and stretched our aching backs. The blood red sun was moving across the sky towards the trees to the west. Darkness, and the lurking horrors it would surely bring, was fast approaching. We had a couple of hours at most.

Sgt. McAllister prepped the drum's bung so that it would open and flood the trench. When he was satisfied, he climbed out and looked down the line.

"How did you get the colonel to agree to silence the specimens?" I queried.

"I didn't," McAllister replied. "He was too busy to see me. I convinced one of the corpsmen to help me. We cut the fucker's vocal cords. That constant moaning was driving everybody insane. It was the right thing to do."

"What did the major say about it?" I asked.

"Nothing. He drank himself into a stupor this afternoon. It's how he is coping," McAllister informed us. "He authorized me to prepare the defenses as I saw fit."

"I take it that means we are staying, no matter what happens?" I inquired.

"Looks that a way," McAllister grunted. He paused to look out at the surrounding forest and listened carefully. Everything was peaceful for the moment.

"The major and the colonel have had a parting of the ways, though," he added.

"What happened?" I asked hopefully.

"The major wants to pull back to the airfield. He just changed his mind all of a sudden like. Might have something to do with my report on how low we are on ammunition and such." McAllister lowered his voice and continued. "He and the colonel had a hell of a row, damn near came to blows. You know how irate the old man can get when things don't go his way. The colonel pulled rank on him. He said his work was almost finished and it was too important to interrupt. Ordered the major to stay put until his command is relieved. The colonel actually called him a coward. You shoulda' seen how purple the CO's face turned! I actually thought he was gonna' blow a gasket and have an aneurysm right there on the spot!" McAllister laughed softly.

"Like we could get that lucky," I added.

"After that, the old man started drinking. He'll be as mean as a snake later, but at least it keeps him out of our hair for a while," the sergeant concluded. "Enough gossip, we still got work to do."

We returned to our preparations. Sgt. Price had readied dozens of plastic gallon milk jugs, now filled with diesel. The cargo truck had been loaded with them, and pulled forward to the slit trench. Hard-on and I set them into the trench in pairs, spacing them roughly equidistant; and removing the caps, leaving them open to the air.

Sgt. McAllister had ordered Price and his men to drain all the diesel fuel from every vehicle except for the truck and two of the Humvees. He wanted every available ounce of the liquid in the trenches. We even raided the village store, and placed every flammable liquid remaining in the place into the channel. A lethal mix of kerosene, lighter fluid, ammonia and bleach, cheap rum and vodka, and almost all our whiskey went into the plastic jugs and into the trench. All of the medical unit's rubbing alcohol went in too. If it was flammable liquid, we pitched it in.

"It's a damn good thing beer doesn't burn," Hard-on growled as he set in the booze. He wasn't happy about wasting good whiskey. Finally, the slit trench was ready.

We had reset the trip wires and set our last few flares at the extreme edge of the village. This would be our first warning, and was well away from the flammables. The killing ground between the village huts and the slit trench was clear. Just beyond the trench towards us, we pounded stout wooden stakes into the ground, and strung out the last of our trip wire between them. A few feet beyond the wire, we drove sharpened stakes into the ground, in staggered rows. The hope was that the zombies might trip and impale themselves, rendering them at least temporarily immobile. Lastly, we set a few long, sharpened poles at a forty-five-degree angle in a hedgehog just before our foxholes. I reflected that soldiers had been doing this same work for centuries, back to the beginnings of warfare, and probably bitching about it for just as long.

Everyone pitched in to shore up our defenses. The mechanics and medics worked just as hard as we did; their lives depended on them, too.

Sgt. McAllister stalked back and forth down the line, looking for weak spots and shouting encouragement, driving us back to work when we slacked or faltered. His deep voice bellowed out above the pounding of the mallets, sledgehammers, machetes, and shovels.

We had done everything we could. McAllister did one final walk around and called it a piece of work.

"It's crude, it's rude, it's pathetic, but it beats a blank. Good work, gentlemen."

Each of our foxholes had been cleared and deepened. Each had been stocked with a half dozen Molotov cocktails, the last of the gasoline in a glass whiskey bottle with a bit of rag stuffed down the neck. You just lit the rag and tossed it at whatever you wanted to burn. Each of us had five hundred rounds of ammunition, twenty magazines each. Once that was gone, well, we all knew what would happen then.

Sgt. McAllister had set up a SAW in the two diametrically opposite corners of the box. Each could fire down two sides of the perimeter. The ammo would last longer utilizing two heavy machineguns instead of four. He set back three M27 linked belts of 556 ammo and another SAW in the center, as an emergency reserve.

At each of the other corners, he had set a single Claymore mine, wired back to the corner hole. The man in the corner hole could trigger the mine by pulling its cord. They also had two grenades each.

We had set up an improvised defensive position around the command tent. It was just a small square made up of empty crates, barrels, and four of the abandoned Humvees as a last resort. Everyone was to fall back on it if we were overrun again. The two fueled Humvees and the cargo truck were parked directly adjacent to this area, ready to go.

The remaining mechanics and the medics went into the lines to fill the empty foxholes. Each had an M-4 with two full magazines, fifty rounds each. McAllister had set the rifles to single shot and warned the men not to change the selector switches back to auto. The remaining Berettas and nine-millimeter ammo had been distributed to them also.

I could tell they were shit scared. I didn't blame them; I just hoped they wouldn't bolt.

We had exactly enough people to fill the foxholes and corners, that was it.

1st Platoon faced the village, 2nd Platoon faced the forest. We all faced death.

Only the old man, Col. Warren, and a couple of lab techs weren't in the lines. Even Lt. Beckham walked out and asked the sergeant where he should post up. McAllister slapped him on the shoulder and sent him over to command 2nd Platoon. Sadler would be the SAW gunner on that side of the world and Sgt. Price would be the gunner on our side. Sgt. McAllister would be in command.

The sun set in a blaze of crimson against the gently waving canopy of the giant trees. No zombies had wandered in while we finished our defenses. There either were no more left, or much more likely, they were massing under the trees, slowly moving forward through the forest, drawn to us like iron filings to a magnet.

My money was on the later.

It grew still. The night was still warm, and the place still stunk, but I was too tired to care anymore. I sat back against the rough dirt wall of my foxhole and closed my eyes for a precious moment. Nothing was trying to kill me just this second. I heard someone laugh, on the other side of the camp. The birds chirped, the insects droned, the night came on. I wished I could just go to sleep and wake up back home, far away from the Congo.

"Hey, asshole, you awake over there?" Hard-on shouted to me.

I stood up in my hole and leaned my ass back against its rim.

"Yeah," I replied. I looked over at him and Gordo. We were the middle of the line. I rubbed my eyes and twisted my head from side to side, trying to work out the kinks and knots in my neck and shoulders. I stretched and yawned.

"You look like shit," Gordo observed dryly.

"He's looked worse," Hard-on observed.

"Kiss my ass," I replied.

It grew steadily darker. The light began to fade away.

"Do you think they'll come back again?" Gordo asked.

I didn't answer for a moment. I just stared out at the empty village and the towering trees. I tried to imagine it before all the death, before the virus. I tried to imagine the people who had lived there before they died.

"Yeah, they'll be back," I finally replied. "They can't help themselves."

Darkness settled down over the village like a funeral shroud. All of the animal and insect noises faded away and it grew still. No one was laughing or talking now.

A tension filled the air, a waiting, a sense of apprehension. A cold chill ran through me despite the oppressive, stifling heat. I could feel them out there, slowly moving forward towards us like an inexorable wave of death and destruction. I tried to remember that they were just human beings like me once.

My throat went suddenly dry and I felt an overwhelming urge to urinate. I ignored them both. I strained my eyes against the darkness, seeking a target.

Abruptly, the eerie moans of the undead broke the silence, all around us. Gunfire broke out on the other side of the square.

"Hold your fire! Wait for a clear target!" Sgt. McAllister bellowed out of the darkness. I eased my finger back off the trigger. I took a deep breath and forced myself to relax. Now that I knew they were here, a calmness overtook me.

The unearthly moans grew in pitch to a nerve-shattering howl. I was sure the zombies had somehow cleared the flares; it sounded as if they were right on us.

"Wait for it! Conserve your ammo!" McAllister warned.

The zombies hit the wire as they stumbled out from between the huts. Two flares sprang to sputtering life, illuminating the advancing horde of undead.

"Fire!" the sergeant screamed.

I leaned forward in my hole and rattled off short, controlled bursts at the shambling horde, switching from one target to the next as they crumpled under my withering fire. The bolt of my rifle locked back far too quickly. I was empty. I mechanically dropped the spent mag and slammed in a fresh one. I threw the bolt and opened fire again.

Dozens of the disgusting, rotten monstrosities surged forward. They clambered and shuffled over the shredded, shot-up corpses that littered the killing ground. The smell washed over me in a fetid wave as they advanced. I fired off one magazine after another as the festering, putrid, walking cadavers came on.

They were incredibly tough. One zombie took a full dozen hits without stopping. I poured the bullets into its frame, walking the rounds from its waist up to its head. Each hit blasted away a chunk of rotten, soggy flesh. The horrible travesty of a human jerked and twitched grotesquely, staggering and stumbling towards me before finally collapsing into a twitching, gibbering mass of shredded red meat. Even then, it struggled to rise and claw its way forward.

The SAW fired from my left. Its tracers and ball ammo walked across the zombies that went down, shredding them into bloody, jerking giblets of flesh and shattered bone.

Still, the zombies came on. There were a lot more of them.

Dozens poured forth from the village and the forest. We could not stop them. There were too many to shoot.

They poured forward over the shot-up pieces of their destroyed kindred and hit the slit trench. The zombies dropped mindlessly into the trench, one after the other. They attempted to climb out, only to be trodden down by the zombies who fell into the pit behind and beside them. The pit began to fill up. A few zombies cleared it by walking across the undead struggling to escape. I concentrated my fire onto them, driving them back.

Sgt. McAllister leapt forward to the fifty-gallon drum. He hit the bung with his shotgun butt, knocking it clear. Diesel fuel gushed into the pit, sloshing over the struggling zombies to either side. They reached out to grab the sergeant, but he was already backing away, firing his shotgun into their outstretched hands. He emptied the gun and pulled a phosphorus grenade from his belt. McAllister pulled the pin and lobbed the explosive into the trench. He dove headlong for the corner foxhole.

The grenade went off with an earth-shaking concussion as the cascade of glowing white-hot phosphorus ignited the diesel fuel. The burning liquid roared through the trench from corner to corner, engulfing each pair of jugs in a raging, twirling inferno of flame. The entire trench erupted into a blazing wall of fire and smoke. Tiny burning droplets of flaming liquid rained down on my unprotected arms, and smoldered in my hair.

The zombies caught in the trench went absolutely berserk. Those that could pulled themselves free and ran like human torches helter-skelter. Most of them hit the trip wires and went down onto the stakes, where they twitched and burned. Some ran back into the forest and the village, setting the huts ablaze. The zombies who couldn't escape sank down into the flaming trench, thrashing wildly as they slowly burned and melted. The smell of smoldering, rotten meat overwhelmed me. I vomited until my throat bled. Acrid, thick black smoke swirled over the line and all around me, blinding me and stinging my eyes. I couldn't breathe or see. I struggled to recover.

I splashed water into my eyes and gulped my canteen dry. I could see that the flames in the slit trench were dying down. More zombies were struggling into the channel, and attempting to climb out the other side. The flames didn't deter them.

In a panic, I slapped my pants pockets until I found my lighter. I lit a pair of Molotovs and tossed them at the zombies nearest me in the pit. The bottles shattered, drenching the already smoldering undead in fresh fuel. They burst into flame, and staggered back to drop down, sizzling onto the blackened, smoking remains littering the trench. Up and down the line, everyone methodically tossed their Molotovs into the channel. They didn't even have to be lit. The flames leapt back up momentarily. Still, more rotting cadavers advanced from the burning village and approached the perimeter. I tossed in my last Molotov and brought my rifle back up.

I fired controlled bursts at the zombies who cleared the slit trench, shooting out their knees and dropping them back into the burning inferno.

For a precious moment, the slit trench held. The flames roared and leapt to the sky. The zombies tumbled forward into a fiery slice of hell on earth, where they were destroyed, incinerated, and cremated. I gave out a ragged cry of victory.

It couldn't last. The fuel burned down, and the consumed dead smothered the flames. Still, more zombies advanced through the smoke and the swirling ashes.

I heard the Claymore go off on my right. The zombies staggered over the stakes and the trip wires. They fell, impaled themselves, tore themselves free, and came on again. The gunfire became sporadic as one by one the M-4's ran dry. I could no longer hear the SAW's automatic fire.

I checked my hip pouch; there were only two loaded magazines left.

A disemboweled zombie lunged toward me, impaling itself on one of my stakes. The sharpened pole tore through its ribs and stuck. The cadaver slowly pushed itself forward, impaling itself further as it reached bony claws towards my face. I aimed and fired off a point-blank burst that decapitated the zombie and took off both its arms. What was left quivered on the pole.

As I reloaded, I looked through the swirling smoke down line to my right. Gordo leapt from his hole and ran back to the center, a cadaver hard on his tail.

I could see Hard-on fighting hand to hand with a zombie. He drove the corpse to its knees with a sledgehammer, and then crushed its skull with a savage overhand stroke. Before he could recover, two cadavers stumbled forward into him. They went down in a tangle of thrashing limbs and then the smoke obscured my view.

A grenade went off directly to my left. I was tossed to the side, shrapnel buzzed by me. Zombies began to emerge from the smoke all around me. I staggered back to my feet, and fled for the center.

I ran back to our last ditch position, passing a pair of limping cadavers that reached out for me as I passed. If we hadn't been overrun, then I was a Chinese jet pilot.

A handful of survivors were assembled behind the barricades. I scrambled up a pile of crates and collapsed inside. I still had my M-4 and about fifty rounds.

It was pure chaos.

I painfully stood up and looked around. I only saw Gordo, Sgt. Price, and a couple of guys I knew from 2nd Platoon, Smith and Jacobs. A pair of the medical guys and one bloodied mechanic staggered in. Nobody was in charge; the survivors were just shooting at the zombies as they approached.

"Where's the sergeant?" I asked Price.

"He's still out there somewhere," he gasped back.

Gunfire broke out from three sides as the zombies approached our position.

The major appeared out of nowhere, screaming contradictory orders. His uniform was crumpled and he looked like shit. He singled out the corpsmen.

"You two, load up our survivors from the sample tent, we're pulling out!" he bellowed.

"What, sir?" one of them stammered back.

"You heard me!" the major screamed. "Go into the sample tent and evacuate all of our personnel. Load them on the truck. We're leaving. Do it now!"

The corpsmen rushed off.

"The rest of you lay down suppressive fire until we are loaded and ready! We only need a few minutes," he urged.

I figured the old man had lost it, but at least we were leaving. He sent a man into the clean tent to bring out the colonel and his staff. He walked over to the barricade and fired off a magazine from his pistol into the approaching zombies, laughing manically.

I heard the distinct noise of Sgt. McAllister's shotgun, and then he leapt over the crates and fell inside the barricade. I had never been so happy to see anyone in my entire life. I helped him to his feet and hugged him.

"Get off me, Parsons," he said gruffly. He reloaded his shotgun and looked around. The major stalked over to us.

"Sergeant, we are leaving," the major repeated.

"'Bout time, sir." McAllister grinned.

Just when I thought we might get out with our skins, the colonel appeared. I didn't recognize him at first. He looked like a mad scientist from an old horror movie. His lab coat was stiff with dried blood and gore. Dark circles stood out under his bulging eyes like old bruises. He was absolutely wrecked. His face was a mask of rage. I could tell he was super pissed.

"Who gave the order to evacuate?" he roared.

"I did," the major replied calmly. He stepped up to meet the colonel.

"I might have known it was you, Dorset," the colonel growled. "I will not allow your cowardice to jeopardize my work!"

The major leaned forward, his hand tightened on his pistol. "Do not call me a coward again, Warren!"

The colonel ignored the major and looked around. "You men will go back to your defensive positions and secure this camp!" the colonel barked. "No one is to leave until you are relieved!"

"We are overrun!" the major screamed back. "Look around you, Colonel Warren! These men are all that are left!"

The colonel shook his head. "Nonsense. Secure the defense of this camp, Major. I must finish my work. Do not disturb me again or

I will bring you up on charges of dereliction of duty!"

Sgt. McAllister grabbed his arm and jerked him around. "With respect, sir, the major's assessment is correct. If we do not withdraw, we'll all be killed."

Warren pulled away. "Stand down, Sergeant!" he ordered. "I want you men back out on the perimeter, now!"

Everyone looked at the colonel in shock. Even the men on the barricade stopped firing for a moment to listen. We could all hear the zombies tearing at the flimsy barrier.

Sgt. Price fired off a burst from his M-4, decapitating a zombie that was attempting to climb the barricade.

The colonel screamed over the gunfire, "Everyone out to the perimeter! Secure this camp!"

Maj. Dorset lifted his gun and calmly shot him three times in the chest. The colonel collapsed to the ground, dead as a mackerel. The rest of us were too stunned to react.

The major lowered his smoking pistol and looked around.

"The colonel was obviously infected with the virus, and had become dangerously insane. I was forced to shoot him in self-defense. Does anyone remember any other version of these events?" he barked. He looked around at us; he still had six rounds in his pistol.

"No, sir!" Sgt. Price replied quickly.

"Very well. Load up. We are the fuck out of here!"

We ran for the trucks.

REPORT FROM MAJOR DORSET CO BRAVO COMPANY

COLONEL WARREN KIA

HAVE EVACUATED VILLAGE OF LAT AND PROCEEDING TO
AIRFIELD.

SPECIMENS SECURED

PROCEEDING AS ORDERED

TRANSMISSION ENDS

MAJOR DORSET US ARMY

CHAPTER 11

09:22 p.m. Zulu
Village of Lat
The Congo

Sgt. McAllister brought up the rear as we withdrew. He had me collect up all the gear we could quickly salvage, and toss it into the last Humvee. He fired off rapid bursts from his shotgun, blasting the clambering zombies who tried to climb the barricade. The buckshot knocked the undead off balance; they tumbled back off the wall. They began to push through the crates and debris; as their numbers grew, the barricade crumbled.

Finally, everyone was aboard a vehicle. Sgt. Price drove the lead Humvee out of the camp. The major climbed into the cargo truck. It pulled away before he could even shut the door. I jumped into the last Humvee and fired up the engine. Tents collapsed as I backed the vehicle through the barricade. McAllister leapt inside and slammed the door. I raced away from the village, weaving through zombies who emerged from the overrun camp all around us. We drove away from the doomed village and into the relative safety of the forest.

I steered the Humvee down the rutted jungle road as fast as I dared. We caught up to the other survivors quickly.

"I can't believe I actually got out of there alive," I laughed.

"We ain't on the planes yet," Sgt. McAllister replied.

We drove through the pitch-black rain forest. The tree trunks flashed by on either side in my headlights, but we spotted no zombies. We had left them in our rearview. I relaxed just a little.

"What are we going to do about the major?" I asked.

"Not a damn thing," McAllister answered. "That was the best thing in the world that could have happened for you."

"But he shot the colonel in cold blood," I retorted.

"Why do you care all of a sudden, Parsons?" the sergeant asked.

"You got exactly what you wanted. If the old man still wants to put you in Leavenworth, at least you've got some leverage on him. Let it go."

I realized he was right. He usually was.

We had covered about ten miles when they hit us. We were running tight, just trying to get back to the airfield. Sgt. Price stopped the lead vehicle hard. A huge tree was down across the track. We bunched up behind him. I slammed on the brakes to keep from hitting the cargo truck in the ass.

Before Price could even get his door open, a rocket-propelled grenade streaked from the trees on our left. The lead Humvee exploded with a deafening roar. It jumped off the road and flipped, awash in flames.

"RPG!" McAllister screamed. He elbowed my hands away and hit the gearshift, throwing the vehicle into reverse. I snapped out of my shock and floored the truck. We accelerated away from the ambush.

Small arms fire erupted from the forest on either side, raking the cargo truck. I saw its brake lights go out and then its reverse light came on. It pulled back towards us, weaving erratically. I craned my head around, trying desperately to keep the Humvee on the track.

A few stray bullets hit our front end; one cracked the windshield, but no one was hit.

We backed around a tight corner, out of the fire.

"Slow down, wait for the others," McAllister ordered.

I reluctantly eased off the accelerator until we were creeping back the way we had come. The cargo truck slewed around the corner and sped towards us.

I flashed my headlights at the driver. He stood on the brakes, barely missing me. We retreated about three miles back down the road. Finally, McAllister ordered me to stop.

We pulled to the side of the track and bailed out of the trucks. Flashlights pierced the darkness.

McAllister ran forward. One of the men from 2nd Platoon had been shot through the thigh. The others helped him out, and the sergeant worked to stop the bleeding.

Maj. Dorset walked back and forth on the track, screaming obscenities at the forest.

He moved towards the others. "Why did they fire on us?" he asked. "Someone answer me!"

McAllister looked up in exasperation. "Sir, this is Africa. They don't need a reason. You definitely offended their leader when we forced our way into the village. They have probably been waiting us the whole time; they knew we would have to come back up that road," he explained.

I walked slowly forward toward the other survivors. Counting the wounded man, there were only ten of us left, half of them noncombatants. Sgt. Price and the other mechanic had died in the RPG attack.

McAllister finished stabilizing the wounded man by wrapping a compression bandage around his leg. He looked up as I approached.

"Get the gear out of the Humvee," he growled. "We are walking out."

The major stomped over. "What?" he demanded.

"We have to walk out, around the rebels," McAllister explained. "It is our only chance."

"We can't leave the vehicles; it is a good twenty miles to the airfield," the major stated.

"Sir, the road is now completely impassable. We can't go forward into another ambush, and we can't go back to the village. We have to circle around the rebels to the airfield. They won't expect us to take to the forest. We should be able to slip past them," the sergeant explained. He poured water from his canteen over his hands to wash the blood away.

"We can't just wander off into the rain forest, Sergeant. It's dark and we'll lose our way," the major complained.

"I've got a map and compass, and my GPS," McAllister countered.

The major digested this for a few seconds. He seemed indecisive. "Fine," he relented.

He walked to the rear of the cargo truck.

"We will take as many of the survivors with us as we can carry," the major snapped. "You corpsmen, unload the stretchers."

The medics walked slowly to the truck and began to unload the struggling zombies still strapped to their stretchers.

Sgt. McAllister shook his head in disbelief.

"Sir, we can't carry those things twenty miles through the brush," he growled.

"We can, and we will," the major retorted. "That's a fucking order, Sergeant."

I could tell that McAllister was close to the breaking point. Even he was not believing how crazy this order was.

"Sir..." he began again.

"Sgt. McAllister, I have just issued you a lawful order. Do you feel that this order is in any way unlawful?" the major asked calmly.

"Not unlawful, just insane," McAllister responded. "We can't carry them that far. They will slow us down to a crawl, and there is no reason to take them. They're not survivors; they are fucking dead, sir! And not just dead, but dead weight. I honestly don't understand what you are hoping to accomplish with this, sir."

"I will not return without them," the major grated. "We were sent here to rescue these men. We will take them home!"

McAllister considered this for a long moment. "Alright, I reckon we can carry two of them, but that's it. We can switch out in pairs, and somebody has to stay on point. There's exactly nine of us, not counting Smith, there, with a bullet in his leg. You'll have to carry some too, sir."

The major smiled. "Excellent, Sergeant. That's the spirit." He pointed to the two nearest cadavers. "We'll take these two brave men home."

McAllister walked back to the Humvee. He pulled me along.

"Let's get what we can carry," he suggested.

"What was that all about?" I asked.

"I don't know what to make of that," the sergeant responded. "I think that somehow the major feels like we need to at least bring something out, so that the mission doesn't seem like such a complete failure."

We rummaged through the vehicle. The sergeant grabbed the last SAW and its remaining ammo. He stuffed our last grenades and Claymores into a sack, and slung it over his shoulder.

"You want me to carry some of that, Sarge?" I asked.

"Naw, I got this shit. You take the mobile radio, and carry all the spare water and food you can. We'll need it before we get to the field. It'll take us two days to get there, maybe three."

I grabbed some MREs and as much water as I figured I could haul. I shrugged on my pack. It weighed at least sixty pounds.

Sgt. McAllister opened the hood of the Humvee. He jerked loose the battery cables, then pulled out his knife and sawed through the main wiring harness at the firewall. He walked forward and repeated the operation on the cargo truck.

"Do you think that's wise, Sergeant?" Maj. Dorset asked.

"I'm not leaving them for the rebels, sir," he countered. "Trust me; we ain't ever coming back here."

We reformed our sadly depleted group. The four remaining corpsmen picked up the stretchers. At least they were used to this shit. I wasn't looking forward to humping a zombie on a stretcher through the woods all night long. I knew it was going to suck.

The sergeant briefed us in a low voice, "Cat's eyes, everyone follow the man ahead of him, stay tight and quiet."

McAllister gave a band to the rear corpsman on each stretcher. He had remembered to bring them along, just in case. He was good at that shit. Combat troops already had them on the back of our helmets or hats. The tabs glowed a faint green, just enough to follow in the darkness. They didn't keep you from tripping over roots and falling into mud holes.

The sergeant continued, "We'll march until I'm sure we've gotten clear of the rebels, then we'll rest until first light."

McAllister strode out ahead on point and didn't look back. He was the only one who knew where he was going.

The major pointed after him and ordered us to march. We fell into a line with the stretchers in the middle. Gordo and I joined the dejected little parade as we moved off into the rain forest. Smith hobbled along behind us as best he could. I looked back at the struggling corpses we were leaving behind on their stretchers in the road and shuddered.

Ten steps off the track, the forest closed in on all sides. We plunged into the darkness and slowly felt our way forward. Sgt. McAllister led us away from the road, east towards the Congo River. The rebels would not expect us to go that way. I continually tripped and stumbled over rocks and roots. I followed the man ahead of me; his tab bobbed up and down in the darkness, a faint green blob of light.

We struggled on through the rough terrain. At least the ground was fairly flat and level. I quickly began to sweat. I smelled almost as bad as the zombies we had been fighting. I was thirsty and hungry and absolutely miserable. I slowly ate a cold MRE packet of chicken noodles as I stumped along. I ended up wearing more of it than I ate. My pack straps dug into my shoulders mercilessly, and my legs hurt like a bitch. Just when I thought I couldn't take it anymore, we stopped.

I plopped down with a groan and drank some very warm canteen water. I wished in vain for an ice cold beer. After a few minutes, the sergeant walked back down the line. He told me and Gordo to switch out with the corpsmen, my pack for the stretcher. I was too tired to complain.

I gratefully gave my heavy bag to the medic and walked forward. Gordo and I lifted the stretcher. The fucking zombie thrashed back and forth, jerking the handles in my hands. You have to carry a stretcher to truly appreciate it. After five minutes, I was ready to pitch the fucker into the brush and take the ass ripping, but I gritted my teeth and sucked it up.

Gordo and I staggered along, pulling and pushing against each other as our footing changed with the ground. I went down hard as I stepped into a mud hole. The stretcher got away from me, and Gordo cussed me for a clumsy bastard. I climbed out of the clinging mud and retrieved our passenger. We lifted him with a groan and staggered onward. The time, we carried the zombie extended out into one long, agonizing stretch of pulled muscles, twisted ankles and banged-up shins. I pushed myself beyond the limits of pain and strength.

I didn't remember stopping, but Gordo had dropped his end. He came forward and helped me lower the stretcher. The line had stopped for a rest. I staggered over to a nearby tree trunk and collapsed gratefully back against it. My arms were numb, and my back was a twitching mass of spasms and pain. I stretched and rubbed my arms and legs, trying to work out the cramps. I was there for maybe ten minutes before the corpsman came back with my pack and dumped it at my feet. He and his partner slowly lifted the stretcher and painfully limped away with it. I struggled back into my pack with a groan, and followed them down the trail.

We moved slowly east as the night wore on. The sergeant kept us going in the right direction. We were all dead on our feet, and it seemed that the nightmare of walking through the dark rain forest would never end. Finally, McAllister felt we were in the clear and we stopped.

Everyone just plopped down wherever they were, with groans and general cursing. I dropped my pack and leaned back against it. The sergeant walked up and down the line, making sure we were all there. Smith limped in last, his leg had gone completely rigid; it was all he could do to walk on it. He sank stiffly down at the end of the line, and lay there groaning softly. I was asleep before I even closed my eyes.

I may have slept for three hours before Smith's screams woke me up. It was still pitch dark, and I was completely disoriented. I had no idea where I was. I snapped bolt upright, clutching my rifle and straining to see into the pitch dark around me. The zombies had found us, I could smell them. Smith screamed again, he was very close.

I jumped up as the sergeant ran past me, a flashlight in hand. He stopped abruptly as the beam illuminated Smith's body.

A pair of rotten cadavers had crept upon him in his sleep. One was ripping bloody chunks from his injured leg with its blackened teeth. The other was cradling Smith's head in its bony hands as it devoured Smith's face. The wounded soldier screamed mindlessly as the zombies slowly ate him. His good leg kicked and twitched uselessly in the mud.

I slowly approached, too shocked to speak.

"Here, hold this on 'em," McAllister commanded me, passing me his flashlight.

The sergeant stepped up to the monsters. He raised his shotgun and blasted the zombies' heads and upper arms away, pumping and firing the shotgun until they were shredded into a twitching crimson ruin. Smith was hit also, but he continued to scream horribly. The sergeant stepped back and pushed a fresh shell into the gun. He racked the pump and raised it for a final mercy shot.

The major moved forward out of the darkness and pushed the gun barrel to the side.

"Don't shot him, Sergeant," he ordered.

"It's too late for him, Major," McAllister growled back. "Let me put him down."

"No," the major replied coldly. "Leave him. His screams will attract the other zombies and buy us some time."

"Fuck you, Major," McAllister growled, raising the gun.

"Don't fire, Sergeant, that is an order," Maj. Dorset commanded calmly. "Listen, out there."

Over Smith's screams, we could hear the dim moans of more zombies, approaching through the trees.

McAllister slowly lowered his shotgun. "Let's move out."

We reformed the column and fled into the trees. I could hear Smith's tortured screams through the trees for a long time. I covered my ears, but the sound haunted me even after I couldn't hear it anymore.

McAllister now led us to the south; we were trying to reach the airfield as quickly as possible. Somehow, the zombies had followed us through the forest and found us in the darkness.

Gordo caught up to me and grabbed my arm. "How did those fuckers find us?" he hissed in fear.

"I don't know," I replied.

"We are moving slower than they are," he pointed out. "They are going to catch us."

"Yeah, I figure you're right," I replied grimly. "Don't worry, the sergeant will figure something out."

We struggled on through the forest, trading out with the corpsman every fifteen to twenty minutes. The stretchers became heavier each time we switched. I didn't think I could keep up the pace. Our line became stretched out dangerously, but I noticed that I could see further into the trees. The sun was rising.

We struggled up a small rise and down into a muddy valley that stretched out between the giant tree trunks. McAllister brought us to a halt.

"Everyone stay put," he commanded. "I'll be right back."

He disappeared into the trees back the way we had come.

I gratefully sank down and shrugged out of my pack. I was utterly exhausted, but I had no desire to sleep after what had happened to Smith. I sank down in the mud and lay there wheezing and coughing. I sipped some tepid water and tried not to retch it back up. I looked around at the others. The fucking zombies on the stretchers were more active than the poor fuckers carrying them. We were all dead on our feet. I didn't see how we could go on much further, and we still had to go another twelve miles or more to reach the airfield.

The sergeant was gone for about twenty minutes. I wasn't worried about him. I recovered just a little. I struggled back to my feet and tried to stretch my legs.

I looked through the trees. McAllister had walked back to us. He leaned over and spat in the mud.

The major stood up stiffly and walked over.

McAllister slowly turned and looked at us. He laughed grimly, "You fuckers are out of shape."

"What did you find, Sergeant?" the major asked.

"The zombies are behind us, maybe a half mile or so," he replied. "They're slow, but they ain't taking breaks and they're tenacious as all hell. I figure they'll catch us."

"How many?" the major queried.

"I'm not sure exactly, but I'd say around a hundred or more," McAllister responded.

"We can't defend ourselves against that many," the major stated.

"No, sir, we can't. That's why we're leaving the stretchers behind and making a run for it," McAllister growled.

"You'll do no such thing, Sergeant! I am ordering you to carry those stretchers!" the major shouted.

McAllister spat on the ground. "I don't care anymore, Major. I don't give a good rat's ass for anything you say. You're just as crazy as the colonel was. I think this damn virus is making everyone crazy. I'm not carrying those rotten fuckers one more step!"

He gripped his shotgun and watched the major. "I'd keep clear of your pistol, sir," he added.

The major remained stock still. He lowered his voice and calmly continued to speak, "Sgt. McAllister, I have been ordered by the Pentagon to bring those two specimens out with us. We are to extract those two cadavers, put them on the planes, and return them to the nearest medical facility for further study. Those are our orders. I was not to disclose these orders to you or the men, but you leave me no choice. I understand your reluctance to transport the cadavers. You were unaware of the orders, and I will not hold your disobedience against you. I give you my word. If you will help me now."

We all stood in silence. We knew our lives depended on the sergeant's decision.

"Wait a minute, Sarge. Why does the Pentagon want those cadavers?" I asked.

"Shut up!" Maj. Dorset growled at me. "This doesn't concern you!"

"They want the virus," McAllister slowly responded. "They want to make a biological weapon out it."

"Motherfucker," I growled.

"Was this the mission all along?" McAllister asked.

"No!" the major shot back. "I was ordered to rescue the medical unit. I swear it! Once the colonel started going through the computer files we found, everything changed."

"Why should I believe you?" McAllister said.

"Because I'm just following orders, just like you," the major replied. "I don't think anyone knew what was going on until we got in here, and the colonel had a chance to analyze the data."

"If you had orders to extract specimens, then why didn't the colonel pull out?" the sergeant pushed.

Maj. Dorset hesitated. Finally, he spat, "The colonel wanted to cure the virus. He felt it was too dangerous to take it outside the Congo without first isolating an anti-virus. He was the one disobeying orders. I was ordered to extract the specimens. We were overrun; we were all going to die. I saved you men's lives!" the major shouted.

"I doubt that was your first consideration," McAllister pointed out.

"What will it be, Sergeant?" Maj. Dorset finally asked.

"We'll take 'em with us and see how far we get," he answered. "We wouldn't want this trip to get boring now would we?"

We all groaned at the news.

"Mount up," the sergeant ordered. "You're fresh, Major; you and I will carry first."

OPS ORD 9-59

SECURE SPECIMENS AT ALL COSTS

REPEAT SPECIMENS PRIORITY ONE

RENDEVOUS WITH SPECIAL FORCES AIRFIELD

ORDERS END

CHAPTER 12

07:22 a.m. Zulu
The Congo
Central Africa

We took the stretchers in shifts; everybody took a turn carrying one of them. It did my heart a world of good to see the major struggling along with one of his precious specimens. Of course, he couldn't carry it for long; he was too out of shape.

We moved as fast as we could under the circumstances, but we weren't making much speed. We were being pursued, and we all knew what would happen if they caught up to us.

Sgt. McAllister moved along the line, encouraging everyone to keep up the pace. He walked with me for a while and we spoke in low tones.

"If something happens, just keep moving south," he instructed me. "You'll hit the road and that will lead you back to the airfield. Always move to the south. How you holding up for ammo?"

"Not great," I answered.

He handed me three spare magazines.

"Where did you get these?" I asked.

"Smith," he grunted. "I didn't figure he needed 'em anymore."

"Thanks," I replied.

"Whatever," he joked.

We walked along for a moment.

"It's just you, me, and Jacobs from 2nd Platoon," McAllister grunted. "The rest of these fuckers are as worthless as tits on a boar hog," he concluded.

"Gordo is okay," I added.

"He ain't no soldier," the sergeant retorted.

"Why are you telling me this?" I asked quietly.

"When those fuckers catch up to us, we're done," McAllister responded. "I expect you to do your duty, but if you're the last one standing, don't wait around for me."

"Okay," I finally responded.

"You're a pain in the ass, Parsons," the sergeant grunted. He walked back up the line. I figured the shit must be getting pretty serious, he had just told me goodbye.

We struggled on for the rest of the morning, taking the stretchers in short shifts. We were all so fucking tired that we kept on dropping the damn things. It was lucky for them that the cadavers were already dead; otherwise, we would have beaten them to death.

We staggered on and on, slowly moving towards the airfield. As we progressed, our pace began to gradually slow until we were moving at a snail's pace. The sergeant's encouragement and the major's threats and screams couldn't whip any more speed out of us. We had carried the stretchers for miles over rough terrain, and we were done.

Without being ordered to, we all stopped. A few of us broke out MREs and water bottles; the rest just collapsed and lay groaning on the muddy ground.

The sergeant and the major moved away from us and sat on the ground, looking over McAllister's topo map and arguing. I just sat there in a daze and closed my eyes. I wanted to sleep now; I didn't care if the zombies ate me anymore. I was drifting away when I heard the first faint groans. I wasn't the only one who heard it.

"On your feet!" McAllister bellowed hoarsely.

Everyone obeyed; we knew they were close.

The corpsmen snatched up the stretchers and took off at a good pace. I knew they couldn't keep it up.

McAllister brought Jacobs back with him and stopped me as the others passed.

"We'll bring up the rear and see if we can slow the fuckers down," he suggested.

We walked along at a brisk limp. It didn't take long before we had caught up to the stretchers again. Everyone was fading fast. The eerie moans of the undead echoed through the giant trees behind us.

"How in the hell do they keep tracking us?" McAllister asked out loud.

I slapped myself in the forehead, "Sarge, I think we may be able to throw them off," I shouted. "Why didn't I think of this before?" I asked.

"What are you talking about?" McAllister asked.

"The river," I answered. "I don't think they'll be able to follow us if we cross the river. We could go across; move downstream and then cross back to this side again. We'll be moving away from the airfield for a while, but it might buy us enough time to get there before they catch up again!"

The sergeant looked at me and laughed, "You're a fucking genius, Parsons. I'm gonna' put you in for a field commission if we get outta' this shit. You are way too smart to be a grunt."

He pulled out his topo map and his compass again. He oriented himself by turning around until he was facing north with the compass, then he looked at the map, and spun it too. He pointed to his right. "It's that way, about a mile, maybe two."

We caught up with the others, and the sergeant moved to the lead.

"Follow me," he shouted. He jogged ahead and we all fell in behind.

We cut through the trees. The zombies were actually closer now, as we moved perpendicular to them. Their groans grew louder. We pushed on as quickly as our tired legs would take us. All of us carried the stretchers now, one man on each handle. We jogged for our lives.

I saw a glimpse of water through the trees, and then we burst out onto the riverbank.

The Congo River was a broad, swirling expanse of dark muddy water. It was a good distance across to the far bank, and the water's current looked treacherous.

We piled up on the bank and looked across at the safety of the far side.

"Let's go, ladies," McAllister growled. "I'll go first to check the depth."

He held the SAW and its ammo belt over his head and waded in.

The water was not as deep as it looked. We followed, still four men to a stretcher. We held the handles on our shoulders and waded into the river. The current tugged at my waist, and my feet slipped on rocks and sank into the muddy river bottom. It was a struggle to remain upright and not drop the heavy stretcher. We slowly made our way across.

Sgt. McAllister slipped several times, but didn't go under. He slowed to show us the way across. Finally, we all struggled up the muddy bank on the far side and dropped the stretchers, too tired to move further.

The moans had not stopped, and without warning a ragged, decomposing zombie emerged from the trees on the far side. I lifted my gun to fire, but McAllister waved me down.

"Let's see what he does," he suggested.

The zombie spotted us and lurched forward, moaning in anticipation. It slipped down the riverbank and fell into the water with a splash. The creature struggled feebly against the current, and then was slowly washed away. It sank and resurfaced several times as it slowly moved away from us. As we watched it, made unsteady progress towards our side; we realized it would eventually emerge and start to pursue us again.

"So much for that," McAllister decided. "Let's roll while we can."

We got back to our feet and struggled up the bank and into the forest. We followed the river upstream, away from the zombies. Tired beyond comprehension or caring, we simply followed the sergeant through the forest as he led us along. Finally, he stopped and led us back down to the river again. We rested among the trees for a few precious moments.

"Good work back there, Parsons," he said.

I waved his praise away; I was too tired to talk about it.

We picked up the stretchers and McAllister led us across the river, back to the side we had started on. Halfway across, Gordo slipped and dropped his handle. The cadaver went under, dragging me with it. I hung on for dear life, pulling against the current as it fought to carry away the stretcher. I surfaced, gasping and cursing.

The corpsmen pushed the stretcher clear of the water, and we fought our way to shore. Gordo rejoined us, and grabbed a handle. Everyone struggled to climb up the muddy bank and then we gimped off into the forest. We were all soaked and muddy, but the zombies were far enough behind us that we could no longer hear them. We only had another ten miles to go. I completely forgot about the radio.

We painfully wound our way through the trees. Sgt. McAllister had disappeared on point. We stumbled blindly along. It was all I could do to put one foot in front of the other, and stagger forward.

Finally, we hit the wall. One of the lead corpsmen dropped his handle and the whole train ground to a halt. Even the major collapsed, panting in the mud. Everyone fell out.

I staggered back the way we had come a few steps, and stood bent over, holding my side. It felt like I had herniated myself. I lay down in the mud.

Gordo stumbled back to join me. "We're not going to make it are we?" he gasped.

"I doubt it," I answered through gritted teeth.

The major eventually limped back to us. "We have to keep moving," he groaned.

"With all due respect, sir, I don't think that is possible," I replied. "Let's wait for the sergeant at least."

"Okay," the major wheezed. He staggered away from us and collapsed against a tree trunk.

Before I could pass out, Sgt. McAllister walked back to find us. He knelt down beside me. "I might have known," he laughed grimly. "You lazy fucker."

He pulled out his topo map and unfolded it. "Maj. Dorset, sir, could you join us?"

The major shuffled over and sat down nearby.

"I've been thinking over our options," McAllister began. "I know we can't keep humping those bastard heavy cadavers all the way to the airfield like this, we're all too damn tired. But we can't stop to rest; we have to stay ahead of them." He tilted his head towards the forest behind us.

"What do you propose, Sergeant?" the major asked.

McAllister pointed to a spot on his map with one gnarled, dirty finger. "We are only about two miles from this village, a place called Mumban. It's just a flyspeck, and the virus has probably already reached it, but they may have transport there. A truck, a car, a fucking donkey cart, I don't give a shit. We appropriate something to transport the cadavers with. If nothing else, we can make the bastard villagers carry them at gunpoint. Whatever it takes."

"Damn," I grunted. The Sarge wasn't normally like this.

"It's not that far out of our way, and we won't make the airfield anyway. It's our best shot," McAllister finished.

"Excellent plan, Sergeant," Maj. Dorset added.

"I figured you'd like it, sir," the sergeant replied.

The major nodded, oblivious to the sarcasm. The plan was right up his alley.

We had all recovered just enough to pick up the stretchers. McAllister urged us on to one last effort, do or die. We staggered forward, stumbling and pulling against each other. Each man fought a battle with himself not to drop his handle. My hands were bruised and bloody, and I had more blisters than skin. The cadavers jerked and thrashed, making the work that much harder. They seemed to be resisting our efforts with a malicious intent. I hated them. All of my pain and misery found a focal point on them and the major.

The sergeant switched out with each of us, one by one, as we progressed through the trees. He seemed to be everywhere. When a man gave out, he would take their place until they could go on again. I marveled at his strength and endurance. He was at least twenty years older than me.

We moved beyond the pain, beyond the surreal journey through the trees, beyond the real world itself and into a place of absolute suffering and wretchedness. I was being scourged, punished for my uncountable sins.

My arms were twin burning cables of trembling hurt and ache. My fingers were numb, and so was my soul. Each step was a jarring, throbbing jolt of fresh pain and suffering. My legs were wobbly, and my muscles spasmed uncontrollably.

I had never imagined that I could endure this much torment.

We reached the village, but I didn't know it until McAllister pushed me to a stop, and unlocked my bloody hands from the stretcher handle. He eased me down until I was sitting in the mud. It took me a minute to realize I wasn't walking anymore. My legs were shaking uncontrollably, and my back had locked up.

McAllister forced two painkillers into my mouth and had me swallow them with some tepid water. He moved through the line of men, helping them to recover as best he could.

Eventually, I could stand again. I hobbled forward towards the edge of the forest. I could see the sergeant standing there, looking at the village just beyond the tree line.

He looked back at me as I approached, and then forward again. His face was set in a grimace.

I stumbled up to stand beside him.

The Village of Mumban had been burned to the ground.

We all trudged out of the woods to stare at horrors we had come so far to find. The villager's heads had been placed on crude wooden stakes in a circle all the way around the village. It looked as if no one had been spared; man, woman or child. Their bulging, festering eyes stared back at us. Clouds of buzzing, fat bodied black flies feasted on the grizzly remains, and wriggling white maggots lay in squirming piles at the base of each stake. The smell was bad, but I had recently been treated to worse. I would have normally puked, but I was far too inured to the horrors of Africa by now, and I had nothing to regurgitate anyway.

Far more pressing to me at this point was the fact that the village had been burned to the ground. Not a timber or wall remained intact. The charred frame of a truck of some sort sat among the swirling ashes. I hung my head and cried quietly.

"It's all burnt," Jacobs observed sadly.

"Gordo, what is going on here?" McAllister asked.

Gordo stepped forward and softly replied, "The severed heads were meant to be a warning not to go into the village, probably not to enter this area, or go any further into the forest beyond the village. Maybe some of the people here had become sick, I don't know."

"Those guys didn't have the virus," I pointed out. "They ain't moving."

None of the severed heads remained animate.

"This is Africa. Life is cheap here. If one person in this village had become infected, then the whole village may have been killed to stop it from spreading further. I have seen things worse than this," Gordo trailed off.

"Who would cut off kid's heads and put 'em on stakes?" I asked.

"This is the Congo," Gordo replied. "Stop thinking like an American or you will never understand anything."

"Well, we ain't gonna' catch a ride here, that's for sure," McAllister spoke. "Let's pull back a ways and rest for a bit. Maybe I can think of something else."

We retreated into the trees, away from the buzzing of the flies and the stench of the burnt village. We sat the stretchers aside and everyone collapsed.

The sergeant sat to one side, studying his map and smoking a cigar. He looked over at me. "Bring me the radio," he commanded.

I struggled over to him and dropped my pack. I rummaged through it until I found the MSRT. As I pulled it out, a thin trickle of water ran from the case.

"Damn it," I whispered, remembering the river crossing.

"Forget it, Parsons. Catch a few minutes sleep while you can," he suggested.

I stalked away and collapsed on the muddy ground. I gratefully closed my eyes.

The sergeant kicked me awake. I sat upright, grasping for my rifle.

"Easy, son," he warned. "Come on, we're moving out."

I wandered stiffly over to the others who had gathered near the stretchers.

"The track that leads into this shit-hole connects up with the road we came in on," the sergeant explained. "We'll follow it back to the airfield. It's about eight miles, give or take. We'll just have to do the best we can. I can't raise anyone at the airfield, but the radio might be out."

"Why would the radio be out?" asked the major.

"Don't know, sir," McAllister responded. "Shit happens. I can't raise anyone; the problem may be on their end."

"We are totally isolated without that radio, Sergeant!" Maj. Dorset barked.

"I know that, sir; it don't change a damn thing. We been on our own since the beginning," McAllister shot back. "We gotta' reach the airfield. It's just down that road." He pointed to the track.

Once again, we picked up the stretchers and struggled along. We were on a well-worn track on level ground, it could have been worse. It also could have been a far sight better.

For the three-hundredth time, I closed my eyes and wished I was back at home, anywhere but carrying these stinking, decomposing cadavers down a dirt road in the Congo.

McAllister paced by us, heading from checking the rear back to out on point.

I hailed him, "Hey, Sarge, I got another idea."

"Lay it on me," he urged impatiently.

"The zombies back there are following us, right?" I asked.

"Yeah," he replied.

"Why don't we cut these fuckers we're carrying loose? They'll just follow us too," I suggested.

The sergeant actually stopped for a second. Then he shook his head and strode ahead.

"I take back what I said about you being a genius," he stated.

"We can leave 'em gagged and with their hands still tied," I added. "We just untie their legs and let them follow us."

"Yeah, Sgt. McAllister; that could work!" Gordo chimed in.

"No fucking way! It's too dangerous," the sergeant responded.

"You're not thinking clearly. What will they do if we get into another firefight with their brothers out there in the wild? You think they'll climb back onto their stretchers like good little cadavers? No, they'll climb all over us while we are trying to fight or run. Those fuckers still want to eat your face, Parsons. Don't forget that." He walked away from us.

"Come on, Sarge," I called after him.

"Damn, I thought that was a good idea," Gordo said. "I'm willing to risk it."

I shifted the heavy stretcher and groaned, "Me too."

TO THE JOINT CHIEFS OF STAFF – CODE RED COMMUNIQUE

RADIO CONTACT LOST WITH BRAVO COMPANY

LAST REPORTED LOCATION NINE MILES WEST OF INSERTION POINT
DRC

REPORT ENDS

CHAPTER 13

01:47 p.m. Zulu
Outside the Village of Mumban
The Congo

I was beginning to get a strong sense of deja-vu. It seemed like I had been carrying a stretcher forever. The handles were stained with blood, and I had wrapped my shredded hands in strips of cloth.

We plodded down the rutted track. I knew that the airfield was somewhere at the end of this road, but I doubted that we would all make it. The poor bastards with me kept on dropping the stretcher handles. Everyone would come to a violent halt, tripping over the stretcher or painfully running into a grounded handle. I had bruises on top of bruises. I had dropped my handle so many times that I had lost count. The only thing keeping me on my feet were the pain pills.

I knew we were not making good time. Our pace would best be described as a slow, painful limp with frequent stops for rest.

Everyone knew it was just a matter of time before the bastard zombies caught up with us again. It was a race. It reminded me of the story of the tortoise and the hare. I remembered damn well who won that one, and we weren't the tortoise.

Sure enough, I started to hear the moans behind us, very faintly at first.

"Did you hear that?" Gordo asked fearfully.

"Oh yea," I answered. "It was just a matter of time."

The sound drove us on to better speed for a moment or two, but we were just too tired to keep up anything better than a hobble.

The horrible sound grew louder as we pressed along. I gritted my teeth until my gums bled. I cursed and I strained, but I couldn't go any faster.

Then, in a perverse twist of fate, the track began to climb a rise; a chorus of groans to match the dead rose from our column.

"You have got to be fucking kidding me," I whimpered.

We painfully struggled to climb the small hill, straining against gravity and the heavy stretchers. Our speed dropped to almost nothing. Everyone fell, struggled up, and fell again as we climbed the hill. Finally, we stumbled over the top.

Sgt. McAllister was waiting there with Jacobs. He pulled me to the side as we passed. The others staggered on without me as best they could.

"Keep going, you guys, follow the major," he ordered gruffly.

"What now?" I gasped.

"High ground," McAllister replied. "We are going to slow the pursuit and buy the corpsmen some time. Those fuckers will catch us in another ten minutes anyway."

"Can I fire from the prone position?" I asked.

"I don't give a fuck what position you fire from, Parsons," McAllister answered.

I dropped down onto my belly on the crest of the hill, "I love you, Sarge," I whispered.

"Shut the fuck up," he responded. "Selectors to single shot only. Aim for their knees. We are only shooting to cripple them. Try to fire only one shot per target, two at most. Do you fuckers understand me?" he growled. He hit me in my head.

"Yeah, I got it!" I cursed.

Jacobs set up opposite my position with the sergeant in the middle. McAllister sat up the SAW and loaded in a belt of ammunition. He told us to get ready. We could hear the undead approaching; their moans grew steadily louder.

"I'm hoping those bastards will be too stupid to flank us, but we can't count on it," McAllister growled.

From our position, we could see clearly back down the track and for a good distance into the trees on either side. Our elevation gave us a good field of fire. Every minute we could hold the zombies back brought the others that much closer to the airfield.

We lay and waited for our targets to arrive. I was so tired that I almost fell asleep. I probably would have if Sgt. McAllister hadn't kept kicking me in my ribs.

The moaning grew to an unbearable pitch and then they were on us. Ragged, decomposing cadavers streamed out of the trees in a wide spread line below us. They weren't just walking along the track; they were everywhere.

"Fire!" McAllister bellowed.

I concentrated on one target at a time. Hitting a person in the kneecap at one hundred yards while they are stumbling along at an uneven gait is not as easy as it sounds. The red dot scope helped tremendously. I squeezed off my shots slowly, trying to make each one count. I cursed at my shots that missed. Our gunfire echoed through the forest. The noise drew the stragglers on our flanks back in towards us.

Zombie after zombie toppled into the mud on the track and in the forest below us. I worked my way from far right in towards the track, blowing off kneecaps and shattering legs. The crippled cadavers continued to crawl uphill towards us, pulling themselves inexorably forward. I disregarded these, and shot at anything still upright and walking.

I shot through my first magazine and then my second. Some zombies went down with a single shot, others continued limping forward, dragging a shot out leg behind them. I fired each time until my target dropped. I fired through my third magazine and ejected the empty. I looked around below me as I reloaded my rifle.

The forest floor below the hill was littered with crawling, crippled cadavers. I estimated at least a hundred, maybe more. Still more were coming. They staggered up the track towards us.

Jacob's M-4 fired twice more and went silent. "I'm out, Sergeant!" he reported.

"How about you, Parsons?" McAllister asked.

"I've got two mags left," I replied sadly.

"Save 'em," the sergeant grunted. He hadn't fired throughout the engagement, but he had readied the SAW. He hunkered down behind it and waited as the remaining mobile zombies stumbled up the hill towards us, letting them bunch up on the track.

"Come on," he urged. "Come on you stinky, rotten, walking abortions!"

The cadavers had almost crested the hill when McAllister open up with the SAW, sweeping it back and forth in short controlled bursts, shredding rotten flesh and bone. The machinegun rattled through the entire belt of two hundred rounds in less than thirty seconds, but not a single zombie remained standing on the hillside. Legless cadavers slid down the hill or lay broken and crippled where they had fallen. The frustrated moans of the undead rose in an unearthly howl as the gunfire died away.

Sgt. McAllister rose and hefted the smoking empty gun. He paused to admire his handiwork; a scattering of zombies were still approaching far off in the distance.

"Let's go, we did enough damage here," he finally decided. He turned and led us away down the track after the others.

We trotted down the other side of the incline and walked after the others. Without the stretcher, I felt as light as air. I wasn't certain how long we had been engaged with the zombies on the ridge, but I was pretty sure we had shot up the more mobile ones following us. We might have a chance now.

The break had given me a small amount of energy back, but I was still incredibly sore. I knew I was going to pay for this little excursion once I actually got to rest. If I stopped now, I wouldn't be able to start again.

It didn't take us long at all to catch up to the stretchers. They were only a half-mile down the track, maybe less. We found them stopped along the trail; the men were lying scattered alongside the stretchers. The major was at the head of the line, slumped over on the muddy track.

McAllister cursed through his teeth. He walked along the line, kicking everyone awake.

"Everybody up!" he commanded, "Parsons, Jacobs, take the last stretcher. Major, you and I will take the lead!"

Everyone fell back into line with a chorus of groans and loud bitching.

The major complained loudly until the sergeant threatened to leave the stretchers again. That got him moving. The line of bone-weary men stumbled off down the track.

We lurched along at a very slow walk. I had nothing left. I was too numb to care anymore. We quickly switched out with the poor corpsmen. They looked like shit. Everyone was filthy and bloody, our uniforms were caked with the African mud. There was only a little difference in appearance between us and the hungry bastards following us.

Somehow, we managed to travel two miles down the trail before everyone gave out. We simply couldn't go one step further. We had to rest.

I fell over on my back and lay groaning in the mud. My ribs were a mass of sharp pain. It hurt to breathe. I could dimly see slices of the bright blue sky through the canopy of the massive trees overhead.

Sgt. McAllister slowly walked back to the rear and sat down in the track, his shotgun cradled in his arms.

I tried to stay awake, but my eyes slowly shut down and darkness overtook me.

I struggled back to the world of the living painfully. Someone was shaking me violently, but I could barely feel it. I finally opened my gummed-up eyes and tried to shake off unconsciousness. Sgt. McAllister helped me to my feet.

"Listen to me, Parsons," he urged. "Follow this track until it joins the road. Turn south, and just keep going. The road will lead you back to the airfield. Take these." He shoved his topo map and compass into my hands.

"What are you doing?" I asked groggily.

"Keep the men moving until you get there. You have to get the cadavers to the planes. The Special Forces unit should be looking for us. Just don't stop," McAllister instructed me. "Now go!"

He pushed me roughly up the trail. The corpsmen were stumbling away with the stretchers. I limped past the major as he walked back to talk to McAllister. I looked back one last time, and then they disappeared behind the trees.

Sgt. McAllister stood in the muddy track and sadly watched the surviving men of his command slowly limp away. He was proud of them; they had been through a lot and they were still trying to get the mission done.

Maj. Dorset walked back to join him. "Are you sure we can't stay ahead of them?" the major asked pensively.

The burly sergeant spat into the muddy track and growled back, "I ain't gonna' sugar coat it for you, sir. We are well and truly fucked!" He looked back down the gloomy forest track and gave a short harsh laugh. "Those cocksuckers are right behind us. Unless someone drops back and slows 'em down, they'll overtake us in a half mile."

"I don't consider you expendable, Sergeant. I can order one of the other men to do it. Who is the most expendable?" the major asked.

"I'll do it," McAllister spat back. "You other cunts would just fuck it up. I'm tired of running anyway, that ain't how I want to go out."

"Sgt. McAllister, what you're doing is very brave. I will see to it personally that you receive the Bronze Star, and I want..." the major began.

"Go fuck yourself," McAllister interrupted him. "You better get your ass on up the trail, our friends are almost here." He tilted his head towards the track. Groans dimly echoed through the trees.

"Sergeant..." Maj. Dorset began again.

McAllister waved him away and took three steps back down trail. When he looked back, the major was gone. "Fucking officers," he cursed.

The sergeant walked slowly back down the trail until he found a decent-looking position to stage an ambush, and moved off the track. He knew the zombies wouldn't keep him waiting long; he wasn't disappointed.

Sgt. McAllister knelt down in the mud and sighted the SAW over the thick downed mahogany log he was hiding behind. He had barely got into position before everything went silent all around him. He could feel the zombies approaching through the trees and foliage. Although his vision was limited to a few yards off the track by the thick cover, he could hear them moving slowly through the brush very close, and he knew they were flanking him. He also knew he was going to die here, alone in the mud of the rain forest, deep in the Congo. In his direst imaginings, he had never considered this scenario as how he would finally die.

Every nerve and the wildly firing synapses of his brain told him to run. His hands were shaking badly and cold sweat ran down his neck and back despite the tropical heat. He hunkered down even lower and his finger tightened involuntarily on the rifle's trigger.

The zombies were crossing the trail before their stench broke upon him like a physical blow. Without thought he fired the SAW, swinging the heavy machinegun back and forth in a deadly arc upon the writhing figures just yards before him. The smoking gun ran through the entire belt of 556 rounds in seconds as the first zombies were cut to wriggling pieces on the gore-covered, muddy trail.

A second wave of corpses came crashing through the underbrush, drawn by the noise of the gunfire. McAllister slammed in a fresh belt and threw the bolt just as the first zombie reached out rotting fingers for him. The big gun spit fire and lead and the zombie disintegrated into bloody chunks of festering flesh and shattered bones. The burly sergeant spun the gun back and forth, firing blindly at anything that moved. The SAW cut down the approaching zombies and all the surrounding foliage, blasting a semi-circle of utter devastation. He raked the fire through the zombies that were down, removing limbs and heads, until only bloody, flopping chunks remained.

McAllister yanked the red hot gun down from atop the tree trunk and broke open the receiver. The barrel burned his fingers as he slammed in a fresh belt of ammunition. He ignored the pain and reset the gun upon the ground to fire behind him. The sergeant realized the gunfire had totally deafened him. He worked his jaw to clear the ringing in his ears. He couldn't hear but he could still see.

He dropped down into the prone position behind the rifle and fired at any movement. Zombie after zombie emerged from the underbrush and was hammered to bloody pieces by the big automatic rifle.

One final corpse crawled forward from the broken creepers and blindly drew its shattered body forward. Most of the zombie's face had been blown away, as had both legs and an arm. The fuckers were incredibly tough. McAllister pulled the trigger and fired until only a quivering pile of bullet-riddled red meat lay atop the blood-splattered mud. The SAW sputtered and fired its final round. He sadly dropped it; the machinegun was the only thing between him and his own impending death.

The sergeant pulled himself up and ran down the lane of fire he had just laid down. He sprinted past crippled zombies that reached out clutching hands to grasp him, evading death by inches. He broke free of the last clutching corpse and raced down the muddy trail. He wanted desperately to just keep on running; he knew he was in the clear.

Instead, he pulled up short and snatched off his pack. He rummaged through it until he had found the last pair of Claymore mines. He worked frantically to set first one, and then the other mine towards the trail. He trailed out the firing lines and ducked behind a tree trunk just as the first of a wave of pursuing zombies staggered up the trail.

McAllister waited until the last possible second, then he yanked the cords. Both the mines exploded simultaneously, firing hundreds of screaming steel ball bearings into the approaching corpses. The closest zombies were shattered and hurled back in a crimson flash. The zombies further away collapsed, their limbs twisted and broken. Still, they came on, dragging their ruined bodies down the trail. As the smoke cleared and McAllister could see again, even more cadavers approached, trampling the struggling undead under their feet into the blood-splattered mud. He turned and fled further down the trail.

Sgt. McAllister didn't run far. He pulled up short and stood bent over on the trail, gasping for breath. He could escape the zombies following him, but every minute he slowed them bought another minute for the rest of Bravo Company to finish their mission. He wasn't doing this because the major had ordered him to, or even to save the rest of the men under his command. He was about to die because he was a professional soldier, and he knew it was his duty.

The sergeant stood slowly upright and removed his backpack. Rummaging through it he found the last bottle of whiskey and tossed the pack aside. He took a long pull of the fiery liquid to kill the pain.

One last cigar was in his breast pocket. He gently removed it and calmly lit it. He stood smoking his cigar and drinking until the zombies were almost upon him.

McAllister tossed the bottle aside and pulled the pin on his last grenade. He threw it as far back down the trail as he could. He calmly pulled his shotgun up and pushed in his last two shells as the grenade exploded. The zombies caught in the blast radius cart-wheeled off the trail into the undergrowth, and severed body parts rained down into the muddy crater created by the explosion. The pair of cadavers closest to him staggered, but then came on. McAllister emptied the shotgun into their faces. Both of the zombies went down, completely decapitated. Their headless bodies groped blindly along the trail, grasping for the soldier. He pumped the last spent shell from the shotgun. It was empty. He tossed it to the muddy ground and pulled his combat knife.

A fresh cadaver stumbled past the two he had shot. McAllister leapt upon it, driving it to the ground. He sank his knife into its neck again and again, working the blade back and forth in an attempt to decapitate it. Blood spurted as the zombie bit him on his hand, and then again on his forearm. The sergeant screamed in pain as another zombie grappled with him, tearing a bloody chunk of flesh from his shoulder with broken teeth. Leprous feet churned the muddy track all around him. The sergeant laughed mirthlessly through bloody lips as he pulled the cadaver's head from its shoulders. He felt more teeth tear at him as the zombies teemed over him, then the pain drained away. His knife slipped from his nerveless fingers into the African mud, and he felt no more.

TO THE JOINT CHIEFS OF STAFF – CODE RED COMMUNIQUE

VIRUS CONFIRMED IN IMMEDIATE AREA OF CONGO BASIN

CASUALTIES WITHIN ACCEPTABLE RANGE

COMPUTER SIMULATIONS PREDICT LIMITED TRANSFER RANGE, ALL MODELS FORECAST DISPERSAL OF VIRUS CONTAINED WITHIN DRC

REPORT ENDS

CHAPTER 14

04:50 p.m. Zulu
Road to Lat
The Congo

I wasn't sure how long I had been out, or how long we had walked further down the track. We all heard gunfire and then the explosions in the distance behind us. The major ordered us to keep moving; we all knew the sergeant would catch up to us eventually. We trudged along until we just stumbled off the trail and back out onto the road that led to the airfield. Everyone gratefully collapsed as the major brought the line to a halt for a moment of rest.

Maj. Dorset walked over to me. "We need to go that way, right?" he asked, pointing to the south.

"Yes, sir," I responded.

"You've got the map. It's your responsibility to keep us on track," he growled, then stalked away and sat down beside the roadway.

I pulled out the map and unfolded it.

Gordo walked over and sat down beside me. "How much further?" he asked.

I traced our route and checked the scale. "Four miles, give or take," I answered.

"Four miles is a long way," he observed dryly. "Do you think the sergeant will catch up to us?"

I had been thinking about him myself. "I hope so."

The major got to his feet and ordered us to move out.

"We're almost there, men, just a little further!" he prodded.

Everyone slowly got up and moved back into a line. The corpsmen picked up the stretchers and hobbled down the road. At my suggestion, Jacobs took point and I brought up the rear. I had given Jacobs one of my magazines. We each had twenty-five rounds for our M-4 rifles; that was it. The major had his pistol, as did one of the corpsmen. Gordo had abandoned his rifle once he ran out of ammo. We had no explosives and could not call in any support. Our situation was critical; we were completely on our own.

I fell back and followed the stretchers; they were moving so slowly that I had to hold back to stay in the rear. I paused to listen for any sign of pursuit, but I heard nothing as we moved forward on the roadway. I looked back from time to time for any sign of the sergeant. As we progressed, I realized he wasn't coming back. This mission was shit.

I just wanted to get the hell out of Africa.

We switched out carrying the cadavers every ten minutes. I insisted that someone watch the rear; the corpsman with the pistol hung back behind us while I carried the stretcher. We made slow progress up the road. It took us over an hour to cover a mile, and then we were forced to rest again. We fell out along the road. No one stood watch; we just laid down and quit.

I didn't realize what was happening until it was far too late. It was almost dark. The rebels silently walked out of the trees on both sides of the road, and captured us with no resistance. One of them quietly approached and picked up my rifle. I had fallen asleep, everyone had.

I was awakened by a pair of soldiers who roughly held me down and tightened a zip tie around my wrists. They hoisted me to my feet, and pulled me back to the trees.

The older commander we had encountered earlier was there, questioning Gordo. They argued back and forth in Congolese. I couldn't understand them, but the man's manner was not friendly.

I was forced to my knees. As I watched, two men emerged from the forest with five-gallon jerry cans. They approached the wriggling cadavers upon the stretchers, and doused them in gasoline.

The major screamed for them to stop until one of the rebels hit him repeatedly with his rifle butt.

One of them lit a pack of matches and tossed it onto the stretchers. I watched as the cadavers writhed and squirmed; the only noise was the crackle of the flames. I wasn't sorry to watch them burn, I was only sorry that we had failed after so much blood and pain. Greasy smoke rose into the treetops, and the stench of burning flesh filled my nostrils. As the flames burned down, they poured on more gas until the cadavers were still, and only blackened bones lay upon the muddy road.

I was pulled to my feet and forced to march down the road. We were moving to the north, away from the airfield. We stumbled and staggered along the road. If we fell out, we were kicked until we rose and went on. When one of the corpsmen went down and couldn't get back up, he was shot and beheaded on the spot.

At least we weren't carrying the damn stretchers anymore.

Our captors said little to each other, and no one spoke to me. When we were allowed to stop and rest, I stumbled forward to fall over beside Gordo.

When I had caught my breath, I whispered to him, "What did their leader say to you?"

Gordo hissed back, "He said he had warned us, that we could never return. He wanted to know why we were carrying the cadavers."

"What did you tell him?" I asked.

"I told him that the major was in charge; that he wanted to make medicine with them. I told him we were trying to find a cure."

"Did he believe you?" I asked hopefully.

"He said there was no cure. He told me that the sick must be destroyed. Parsons, I think we fucked up. I have been listening to them talk. I don't think these men are rebels at all. I think they are local militia who have established a quarantine zone. They attacked us to stop us from spreading the disease," Gordo explained.

"What are they going to do with us?" I queried.

"Their leader said something about taking us back to a village. I don't know. They want to make some sort of show out of the major; they consider him important. Maybe they will ransom us."

"I doubt it, Gordo," I replied grimly. "Remember, this is the Congo."

OPS ORD 10-02

US ARMY CAPTAIN TUCKER, SAMUEL, J. SPECIAL FORCES

LOCATE AND EXTRACT ACS SPECIMENS PRIORITY ONE

ASSIST AND EXTRICATE BRAVO COMPANY PRIORITY TWO

EXERCISE EXTREME CAUTION, ACTIVE ACS VICTIMS AND REBEL
ACTIVITY IN AREA

ORDERS END

PROLOGUE

06:33 a.m. Zulu
Abandoned Airfield
Democratic Republic of the Congo

Captain Tucker slipped out of his parachute harness and quickly wrapped the collapsed silk in the para-cord. He pushed it down into the tall grass at the edge of the field and looked around him. The rest of his five-man fire team was already moving forward to his position. Tucker scanned the airstrip with his binoculars, but it was still too dark to see clearly. He could see no sign of movement or activity.

His second, Specialist Bradford, moved up and knelt down beside him. "Sir?"

"We wait," Tucker answered.

The Special Forces unit disappeared into the tall grass.

Twenty-five minutes later, the sun had risen enough to see across the deserted airstrip. The three C-130 cargo planes still sat on the field where they were supposed to be, but they would never fly again. Each had been burned. Black scorch marks were clearly visible around the cockpit windows, and their tires were flattened. A partially collapsed tent stood nearby.

Capt. Tucker used hand signals to direct his team forward. Three men slipped forward through the tall grass, and stopped at the edge of the landing strip.

Tucker waited until he was sure they were in position, then rose and silently led the other two forward. They cleared the short distance to the planes, and flattened out against their burned-out hulls. The men they had passed moved rapidly forward and cleared the rest of the airfield. They encountered no resistance, and quickly located the military unit they had been sent to assist.

"Why did they behead them?" Bradford asked through the bandana he held tightly over his mouth and nose.

"I don't know," the captain responded. "Talk to me, Felder."

Their medical officer, Lieutenant Felder, knelt among the pile of badly burned remains they had found at the far edge of the field, near the surrounding rain forest. He slowly stood and removed his surgical gloves, dropping them among the debris.

"Sir, I cannot explain why these men were murdered in this manner. Some were shot and then beheaded; some were just decapitated. Perhaps they had surrendered. I would guess that the bodies were burned afterwards."

He stood and slowly walked to the pile of fire-blackened skulls nearby.

"These were our people, I'm sure of that," he finished grimly.

"How can you be sure?" Bradford asked.

"Their teeth," the lieutenant replied, gently moving a detached jawbone with his boot. "Africans don't have fillings."

"We'll pick them up on our way out," Capt. Tucker said softly. "Let's see if we can find anyone from Bravo Company who's still alive, then we'll get some payback."

Capt. Tucker picked out the tracks of the Humvees near the edge of the airfield. He led his men down the rutted track, following them into the rain forest. They moved as quietly and quickly as six ghosts. Three miles in, they found the burnt remains of two men lying in the center of the road.

Lt. Felder quickly examined them. "Ours again," he reported.

"Damn," the captain growled. "What the fuck went on here?"

The captain scanned the ground around the charred bones. He knelt in the loam near the giant trees at the edge of the track. "Looky here, boys," he growled, pointing to a set of boot tracks in the mud. "These were made by one of ours, and I'm pretty sure he was still alive. He was walking when he made 'em."

He peered at the muddy ground, trying to read the story imprinted in the muddy ground there. "Looks like a bunch of locals, and a few of ours, probably taken prisoner."

"How in the hell can you tell all that?" Felder asked incredulously.

"The ground is so muddy that a child could read the tracks. These boot tracks were heading south up to this point, then they are muddled up with these barefoot prints here where we found these bodies," the captain explained. "And these over here are headed back north, the way they came, all traveling together. Our people would have been making for the airfield, behind us to the south."

"What now?" Felder inquired.

The captain pointed down to the tracks leading north. "We follow these boot prints."

The Special Forces unit carefully followed the tracks along the road for another mile. At that point, they pulled up short.

The captain was on point; he held up his hand to stop the men behind him and motioned them off the road. Tucker had spotted someone looking back down the trail directly ahead of them. The man wasn't moving, and Tucker was sure he hadn't been spotted. He cautiously moved into the trees and slowly made his way forward, looking for trip wires and booby traps as he moved from tree to tree. He slipped forward until he was overlooking the road, and then belly crawled the last few yards until he could peer over the twisted tree roots down the rutted track. Moving with extreme caution, he brought his M-4 up into firing position and peered through the scope until he acquired his target. Slowly, he lowered the rifle. Capt. Tucker had found the men they were looking for. They were mere yards away.

Parsons, Gordo, and Maj. Dorset stared back at him from atop their stakes.

The End

END NOTES

CHAPTER 4

Night Vision Goggles - NVGs
Most military forces now commonly utilize night vision goggles. They simply amplify ambient light to give the wearer an artificial sense of vision. Everything appears in a dim green hue. The drawbacks include a limited field of view (Roughly 40 degrees straight ahead) and a flat two-dimensional sight plane.

MOPP Suits - Mission Oriented Protective Posture
MOPP suits are simply an ensemble of protective gear, including a hooded, rubberized over-garment, a gas mask, booties, and gloves. The number following the word MOPP correlates to the level of threat.
MOPP Level 1 — Suit worn. Mask, gloves, and boots carried.
MOPP Level 2 — Suit and boots worn. Gloves and mask carried.
MOPP Level 3 — Suit, boots and mask worn. Gloves carried.
MOPP Level 4 — All protection worn.
Wearing a MOPP 4 suit is like being wrapped in a thick condom and shoved into an oven on preheat. You have to experience it to appreciate how much it truly sucks. It is a great way to lose weight, however.

IED - Improvised Explosive Device
A homemade explosive set to detonate by trip wire or remote detonation.

CHAPTER 6

MSRT - Mobile Satellite Radio Transmitter
Field portable satellite radios utilized for communications. Although usually carried on Humvees, a combat patrol on foot

would include a radioman equipped with a MSRT.

CHAPTER 10

Molotov Cocktail
As described, a hand hurled incendiary device constructed by filling a glass bottle with a flammable liquid, and stuffing a rag into the neck. The rag acts as a wick, or fuse, when lit. The Molotov is thrown at the target, and bursts upon impact, covering the impact area with flaming liquid.

CHAPTER 11

Cat's Eyes
Small square luminous tabs on an elastic band, worn on the back of the helmet or hat. These tabs glow dimly, giving off just enough illumination to guide the poor tired bastard behind you in the dark. As a joke, soldiers often hold them in hand at the appropriate level and guide the person behind them into a tree or mud hole.

THE CHARACTERS OF BRAVO COMPANY

PFC Parsons
Parsons was drawn to a large degree from my own experiences in the military. I was sometimes too smart for my own good, questioned orders, and got into a bit of trouble with my superiors. If Parson's ass-ripping by the major seems realistic, well, you should have been there.

Hard-on
Harde, or Hard-on, was a straight amalgamation of two guys I met in Air Force Tech School. One was named Bob Evans. He was super cool, and from New Jersey. He taught me the Jersey slang (What exit ya' from?) and how the people there talked and acted. The other was an extreme muscle head asshole (also from Jersey) whose name I honestly do not remember. If those two guys screwed, Hard-on would be their kid.

Jonesy
Jonesy was a mash-up of the poor inner city kids I went to grade school with. He mainly came from my memories of my best friend in grade school, a crazy kid named Craig, who got me into more trouble than I can remember.

Gunner
Gunner came mostly from my imagination, but I met a lot of Hispanics while I was stationed at Homestead AFB, near Miami, Florida. Most were really good people, and I really liked them and their culture. I love Cuban food! Several of them were just like Gunner, and would stomp the shit out of you if you looked at them wrong.

Sgt. McAllister
The Sarge is an amalgamation of all the old, hardnosed, capable, military types I've known over the years. When I first began to write about him and see him in my head, he began to take on a lot of the

145

characteristics of my father. My dad was a true woodsman; he taught me to track and hunt, how to handle a gun and shoot, how to be a man. He was tough as nails, and didn't take shit from anyone. A master sergeant is a lot like a father to the men under his command. He is responsible for them, watches over them, and disciplines them.

Major Dorset
The major was based on a couple of officers I met along the way. I won't name them, because they already know that they are raging assholes. They took pride in being aloof, superior, constipated pricks. Every non-commissioned serviceman out there knows Major Dorset; he was everywhere.

THE WEAPONRY OF BRAVO COMPANY

The modern firearms depicted in *Rotters: Bravo Company* are real. The descriptions below are generic examples of the M-series of firearms produced for the military.

The M-4 Rifle

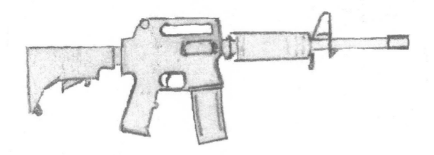

Specifications:
Caliber: 5.56x45 mm
Weight: 6.4 lbs. (2.9kg)
Overall Length: 33 in (840mm)

Magazine Capacity: 30 round box

Capabilities:
Muzzle Velocity: 2970 f/s (884m/s)
Rate of Fire: 700-950 rds./min
Maximum Range: 500 yds (500m)

Squad Assault Weapon - SAW

Specifications:
Caliber: 5.56x45 mm NATO
Weight: 17 lb. (7.5kg)
Overall Length: 40.75 in (1035mm)

Magazine Capacity: 200 rounds on M27 Linked Belt

Capabilities:
Muzzle Velocity: 3000 ft./s (915m/s)
Rate of Fire: 50-775 rds./min
Maximum Range: 870 yd. (800m) effective3940 yd (3600m) max

12 Gauge Assault Shotgun

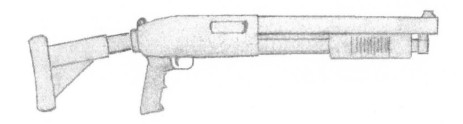

Specifications:
Caliber: 12-Gauge Shotgun (OO Buckshot)
Weight: 5 lbs. (2.3kg)
Length: 40 in (457mm)
Barrel Length: 18 in
Action: Pump

Magazine Capacity: 8 rounds

Capacities:
Maximum Range: 150 ft. (50m)

Claymore Mine - M18A1

Specifications:
Caliber: 700 1/8th inch steel balls
Weight: 3.5 lbs.
Length: 8.50 in (216mm)
Height: 4.88 in (124mm)
Width: 1.50 in (38mm)

Capabilities:
Muzzle Velocity: 4000 ft./s (1200m/s)
Maximum Range: 55 yd. (50m) 250m max

The Claymore anti-personnel mine consists of a plastic case containing a C-4 shape charge behind an epoxy resin containing approximately seven hundred steel balls. It can be detonated by remote control or rigged to a trip wire.
The mine fires forward in a wedge pattern 6 feet high by 165 feet wide at its optimal range of approximately 55 yards, hurling seven hundred steel balls at anything in the blast radius.

Fragmentation Grenade - M167

Specifications:
Weight: 14 oz. (400g)
Length: 3.5 in (88mm)
Diameter: 2.5 in (64mm)

Maximum Range: 30yds (30m) thrown, blast radius 45ft (15m)

The M167 grenade is simply a hollow steel sphere packed with C-4 and a three-second delay fuse.

White Phosphorous Incendiary Grenade M15 (Willy Pete)

Specifications:
Weight: 31oz (88g)
Length: 6 in (152mm)
Diameter: 2.5 in (63.5mm)

Maximum Range: 30 yds. (30m) thrown, blast radius 50 ft. (17m)

The white phosphorous released by the grenade burns at approximately 5000 degrees Fahrenheit. Although classified as a smoke grenade, the Willy Pete can also be used to destroy soft targets, and once ignited, the white phosphorous will burn through almost anything.

ABOUT THE AUTHOR

Carl Cart is an author and award winning independent film maker. He lives in rural Southern Indiana in a small cabin with his wife Jennifer and their dog Bob, patiently awaiting the zombie apocalypse.

Carl is the author of the *ROTTERS* trilogy, and the zombie/comedies *DWARFS OF THE DEAD* & *DETOUR 366*.

For more information, visit the website www.carlcart.com

CHECK OUT OTHER GREAT ZOMBIE NOVELS

900 MILES
by S. Johnathan Davis

John is a killer, but that wasn't his day job before the Apocalypse.

In a harrowing 900 mile race against time to get to his wife just as the dead begin to rise, John, a business man trapped in New York, soon learns that the zombies are the least of his worries, as he sees first-hand the horror of what man is capable of with no rules, no consequences and death at every turn.

Teaming up with an ex-army pilot named Kyle, they escape New York only to stumble across a man who says that he has the key to a rumored underground stronghold called Avalon..... Will they find safety? Will they make it to Johns wife before it's too late?

Get ready to follow John and Kyle in this fast paced thriller that mixes zombie horror with gladiator style arena action!

WHITE FLAG OF THE DEAD
by Joseph Talluto

Millions died when the Enillo Virus swept the earth. Millions more were lost when the victims of the plague refused to stay dead, instead rising to slaughter and feed on those left alive. For survivors like John Talon and his son Jake, they are faced with a choice: Do they submit to the dead, raising the white flag of surrender? Or do they find the will to fight, to try and hang on to the last shreds or humanity?

CHECK OUT OTHER GREAT ZOMBIE NOVELS

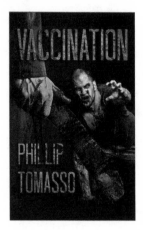

VACCINATION
by Phillip Tomasso

What if the H7N9 vaccination wasn't just a preventative measure against swine flu?

It seemed like the flu came out of nowhere and yet, in no time at all the government manufactured a vaccination. Were lab workers diligent, or could the virus itself have been man-made? Chase McKinney works as a dispatcher at 9-1-1. Taking emergency calls, it becomes immediately obvious that the entire city is infected with the walking dead. His first goal is to reach and save his two children.

Could the walls built by the U.S.A. to keep out illegal aliens, and the fact the Mexican government could not afford to vaccinate their citizens against the flu, make the southern border the only plausible destination for safety?

ZOMBIE, INC
by Chris Dougherty

"WELCOME! To Zombie, Inc. The United Five State Republic's leading manufacturer of zombie defense systems! In business since 2027, Zombie, Inc. puts YOU first. YOUR safety is our MAIN GOAL! Our many home defense options - from Ze Fence® to Ze Popper® to Ze Shed® - fit every need and every budget. Use Scan Code "TELL ME MORE!" for your FREE, in-home*, no obligation consultation! *Schedule your appointment with the confidence that you will NEVER HAVE TO LEAVE YOUR HOME! It isn't safe out there and we know it better than most! Our sales staff is FULLY TRAINED to handle any and all adversarial encounters with the living and the undead". Twenty-five years after the deadly plague, the United Five State Republic's most successful company, Zombie, Inc., is in trouble. Will a simple case of dwindling supply and lessening demand be the end of them or will Zombie, Inc. find a way, however unpalatable, to survive?

CHECK OUT OTHER GREAT ZOMBIE NOVELS

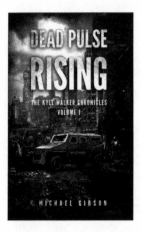

DEAD PULSE RISING
by K. Michael Gibson

Slavering hordes of the walking dead rule the streets of Baltimore, their decaying forms shambling across the ruined city, voracious and unstoppable. The remaining survivors hide desperately, for all hope seems lost... until an armored fortress on wheels plows through the ghouls, crushing bones and decayed flesh. The vehicle stops and two men emerge from its doors, armed to the teeth and ready to cancel the apocalypse.

TOWER OF THE DEAD
by J.V. Roberts

Markus is a hardworking man that just wants a better life for his family. But when a virus sweeps through the halls of his high-rise apartment complex, those plans are put on hold. Trapped on the sixteenth floor with no hope of rescue, Markus must fight his way down to safety with his wife and young daughter in tow.

Floor by bloody floor they must battle through hordes of the hungry dead on a terrifying mission to survive the TOWER OF THE DEAD.

Made in the USA
Lexington, KY
19 May 2019